Stone Guardian:

A Paranormal Protector Tale

Book 1 in the Heart of Steel series

DEMELZA CARLTON

This book was created with the assistance of a grant from the Western Australian Department of Local Government, Sport and Cultural Industries.

ONE

Stanley Steel never forgot the moment he fell in love. He only glimpsed her for a moment — silver blonde hair flying in the breeze as she stuck her head out of the carriage window, her joyful face turned heavenward to drink in the rare rays of Scottish sun.

The next moment, his face was on fire, bleeding from a blow delivered by the riding crop coming down to strike him again. Stan flung up his arms, blocking the second blow with the handle of his shovel.

"That's right, boy, keep your eyes on the ground, where they belong. If you ever raise your eyes to my sister Carline again…" The rider clenched his hand around his riding crop and shook it.

So that was the angel's name. Carline. Stanley liked the taste of it on his tongue. A beautiful name for a lovely lass.

Love made him bold. "It is a public road, sir, and 'tis no crime to look at those who travel upon it. Why, if we do not pay heed to every speeding carriage that comes past, a man's likely to get run over!"

The other men, his cousins all, began to laugh.

The fine gentleman drew himself up, tugging hard on his horse's reins as he did so, making the poor beast dance in a circle. "I am William Steel, and one day all these lands will be mine. And you will work in the muck, from dawn until dusk, until the day you die."

"Steel is it? Well met, then, Mr Steel, for

that is my name, too!" Stan said.

The other men chorused their agreement, for they were all Steels, though younger sons or sons of younger sons, so they'd grown up as farmers, while William Steel, evidently named for the knight who'd built the manor house that ruled over these lands, was a first-born son's first-born.

William Steel snarled, "You may bear my great-grandfather's name, but you are scum compared to my sister and I. Our blood is as blue as the King's own, for we are descended from his first wife, English lady that she was, whereas all of you are descended from the scullery maids the old man bedded and wedded in his grief for his lost lady. Your blood is as murky as the mud you shovel, and not worthy to be mixed with mine or my sister's. If you so much as look at her again, I will have you flogged. And should you even attempt to speak to her...it will be the last thing you ever do."

He kicked his horse, hard, and the poor

beast leaped forward, having more sense than its master as it avoided Stan and headed for the road that the carriage had taken.

Something touched Stan's shoulder. He whipped around to find Wystan standing behind him.

"You should not anger that man, Stan. He's a hard one, they say, and his father sent him to school in England, learning to grind all Scotsmen beneath his boots. If the rents go up much more, none of us will be able to afford them, and we'll have to go work in some factory, or worse, the coal mines. Better to tempt the devil himself than the Steel who'll rule the manor."

Stan didn't care about William, for he could only think of Carline. "Ah, but it's his sister I want to tempt, Wys. Did you see her? A lovely lass who looked like an angel…"

Grant laughed. "You heard him, coz. We're not worthy of angels, or even lasses who look like them."

That's when Stanley Steel vowed he would

prove the man wrong. He was worthy of Carline Steel, and he would make her and her brother see it. One day.

TWO

"No stupid virus is going to keep us from having the holiday of a lifetime."

Alethea winced. "But Mum, the stories we're hearing here about all the sick people in Italy…"

"That's why I persuaded your mum to stay in France for a bit longer. We've found a lovely town with a weekly farmer's market, and one of the lovely snail farmers was willing to let us park our motorhome on her farm for as long as we like. You should see the view across the hills from here. It's just…"

"Lovely?" Mum interrupted, pushing her way in front of the camera next to Dad.

Alethea had to smile. Dad had never been good at superlatives. If she asked him what snails tasted like, he'd probably say they were lovely, too.

"There is talk that they might close the borders, though, and you won't be able to fly home." She didn't want them to come home early – they'd been planning to drive around Europe for years – but the Premier had been adamant that if West Australians wanted to come home, they had to come home now.

"I'm sure they'll be open by Christmas, which is when we'd planned to come home anyway. If it takes any longer, I can always find a job. Everyone needs nurses," Mum said. Her eyes narrowed. "Are you taking proper care of my orchids?"

"Yes, Mum. Watering them only once a

week, and just the right amount of sun." There was a whole page of instructions, and she'd been following them religiously. And here she'd thought housesitting for her parents would be easy, seeing as they didn't have any pets.

"And what about your new year's resolution? Any progress?" Mum prodded.

Alethea sighed. Dealing with delicate orchids was much easier than actually achieving her resolution this year. She probably should have said she'd lose weight or something. Anything would be easier than…

"Because you actually have to go looking for love if you want to find it, sweetheart. Go out to places where you'll meet new people. Then go on dates."

Another sigh escaped. "I want to, Mum, but we're working on a really exciting dig at work and when we're done for the day, all I want to do is shower off the dirt and fall into bed. I mean, it's the first time anyone's done this kind of investigation on a colonial era cemetery before, and some of the stuff we're finding, it's just…" Highly confidential, so confidential the land owner had made them sign all sorts of non-disclosure agreements so they wouldn't share their findings with anyone. "Really exciting," she finished.

"Are there any men your age at the dig site?" Mum demanded.

"Yeah, but…all the exciting ones are dead, Mum." Or already taken.

"Next time I call, I want to hear you've been on a date. An actual date, Alethea Caroline Bell. And I want to hear all the gory details."

Dad paled. "Maybe not all the gory details."

Mum smacked him and he disappeared from view. "Yes, all the gory details. I'm a nurse. Well, a retired one. I saw every kind of gory there is before my meal break, and then saw it all again on the second half of each and every shift. I want to know if he…what does your cousin Callie call it? Oh that's right. If he gives good dick."

Anguished howling from Dad in the

background. Alethea wanted to make the same sounds.

"Mum, Callie only says that to shock people. I'm sure she's never actually said it to someone who's equipped with…" Oh hell, now she was blushing.

"A penis?" Mum finished for her.

No, she was not going to talk about her sex life with her mother. Even if they were video calling her from France, while she hunkered down in their East Perth apartment. "Mum!"

"All right, all right. I'm sure you'll use your good judgement, like you usually do. I mean, you're not Tacey."

"Mum, Tacey's the most responsible out of all of us. As a single mum, she kind of has to be. And she's a business owner…"

"Yeah, but…"

"All right, Mum, I'll do my best not to make the same mistake Tacey did. I won't sleep with an abusive arsehole who'll try to kill me, and I'll make sure to use two condoms, in case one breaks. Happy?"

Mum frowned. "You know what I mean. You're just starting your PhD project. You don't want to mess things up and never finish. Do you know how many people never finish?"

No, and she didn't care, because she wasn't going to be one of them. This cemetery dig was going to give her all the material she needed for her PhD project and a whole bunch of papers.

"Honey, we have to go. Claudine said she's ready to take us on a tour of the farm now," Dad said, tugging at Mum's arm.

Mum wagged her finger at the screen. "A date, Alethea. Promise me you'll go on a date."

"Yes, Mum."

A flurry of goodbyes ended the call, and Alethea's screen went dark. She closed her laptop.

At least she hadn't had to make any promises involving penises.

THREE

"He's put the rents up again. That's the second time in a year. If the price of wool drops any further, we'll have to sell the sheep just to pay rent, and it's only a matter of time before we run out of sheep," Harlow said.

Wystan just hung his head. He'd said little in the months since his wife and daughter had died, even after Stan, Harlow and Grant had moved into his cottage to help him out. All right, they'd moved in as much to save on rent, as one cottage cost less than two, but Wystan hadn't really cared.

Stan shook his head. As always, it would be up to him and Harlow to come up with a solution to their problems. Wystan was no help and heaven only knew where Grant had gone.

There were jobs in the factories, he'd heard. A man could earn an honest living if he was willing to leave the farmland where he'd grown up and move to the city. Or closer to home, maybe he and Grant could take up coal mining, leaving Wystan and Harlow to run the farm. Between them, they might be able to stave off eviction for a while.

But if the rents rose again, as Stan didn't doubt they would, for there were whispers about William Steel and the mighty mortgage he'd taken out on the land he'd inherited from his father…

Grant burst into the cottage, slamming the door open so hard it bounced off the wall and nearly knocked him over. He didn't seem to care, though, for he only rubbed idly at his shoulder as his grin widened.

"You should all get down on your knees and thank me, for I have found the solution to all our problems. A solution so brilliant it will make all our fortunes, and we'll never have to pay rent again, for we'll all be rich landowners in our own right!" Grant threw a slim black book on the table. "We shall all emigrate to America!"

Harlow burst out laughing. "That's a good joke, brother. The only men making money in America now are those who own or sell slaves. Seeing as that's illegal here and even if it wasn't, we have no money to buy anyone, so you surely mean we will have to sell ourselves into slavery to some shady illegal slave dealer you met down the pub!"

Even Stan had to laugh at that.

Grant only pouted. "That is not true! I did not hear it from some stranger at the pub, but from one of the grooms up at the big house.

He found this book in William Steel's own carriage, and there is talk of him letting all the servants go so as he can sell the big house before it drives him bankrupt. What money he has, he plans to buy trade goods to take with him to the colonies. And if the Steels in the big house are doing it, then you can be sure there is money to be made."

"If William Steel is going to America, then I want to be on the other side of the world from wherever he is," Stan declared, flipping the book open. "Either here or New South Wales or..." He squinted at the first page. "Where on God's green earth is the Swan River Colony?"

Grant's grin returned. He took the book from Stan and leafed to the pages at the back. "It's in Australia, on the other side of the island from Sydney. No convicts at all, and they say that every man who arrives there before the end of 1830 gets forty acres of land, with no rent to pay, ever."

Stan's mind spun. Forty acres? That was larger than William Steel's estate here. He seized the book. There must be some catch. No one would give such largesse for nothing. "Ah, but here's the rub! We must invest three pounds for those forty acres. I don't know about you, but we'd be lucky to rustle up one pound between us, if we sold everything we own, and that would barely pay for our passage to this colony."

"You need to keep reading, coz. There's more. Any man who pays for the passage of a labourer will get two hundred acres per man. A certain Sir Thomas Peel has hired two ships to carry men and all that is needed to tame this colony, and he promises to give a portion of his land to every man who signs on to sail with him! Forty acres per single man, after five years of indentured labour."

Indentured servitude. Stan had heard of such things in the Americas, where it was little better than slavery, but with the promise of so much land for only working five years…

In five years, he'd be able to prove himself worthy of Carline. He'd own more land than her brother, free and clear, with no mortgage. That'd show William Steel who was worthy.

"Sign us all up. You, me, Harlow and Wystan," Stan instructed. "Five years of labour for forty acres is a bargain by any man's reckoning. If this Swan River Colony is half as fertile as this book says, we'll be rich men, well able to afford to pay for passage for the rest of our family to come and join us. Or to come back here and buy the big house for ourselves."

Grant clapped his hands. "It sounds like a wonderful adventure!"

Harlow regarded Stan with hard eyes. "It sounds like madness, or a mad gamble, at least. Why should I let such lunacy infect me?"

"Because it's lunacy to stay, or to go. Life is a gamble, and right now, the only choice we have is in the manner of our madness. We may take a gamble on this Swan River Colony, and work five years of our lives for our own land. The work will be hard, to be sure, but to own land is worth it. Or we can stay here, and work our collective arses off, selling sheep and the sweat of our brows until there is none left, and we are evicted. There is no future here. If we stay, we may only delay fate for a little while, but ultimately, we will lose. If we emigrate…one way or the other, we will surely win."

A faint smile touched Harlow's lips. "Ah, a man after my own heart, coz, you know how to win me over. I never gamble unless I know I will win, for I hate to lose. Besides, there's Wystan to think of. The man needs a change of scenery to cure him of his melancholy. A little hard work in this Swan River wilderness might do him good."

Stan drew in a deep breath and blew it out slowly. It was settled, then. To the Swan River Colony they would go, and the devil take the hindmost.

FOUR

Alethea never imagined so much could change in a week. National borders were closed. State borders were closed. She wasn't even allowed to leave the city. Restaurants and pubs and libraries closed, and there was caution tape around the children's playground in every park. Oh, and everyone's hands were raw with the overuse of hand sanitiser, like people had forgotten how to moisturise.

The best part was how you were supposed to stay two metres away from everybody, so you couldn't catch the virus. The one that had killed so many people in Italy and China and she couldn't remember where else, but she'd seen coffins on the news, all lined up, waiting to be buried.

As if she didn't see enough coffins at work. Well, coffin fragments, as the ones she was digging up had been there for more than a century, compacted under first a tennis court and then a car park. Her work, being outside and easy to avoid people while doing it, didn't change. Well, someone had stuck a bottle of hand sanitiser in the lunchroom, but everyone preferred to wash their hands thoroughly instead. Because when you were dealing with human remains, a squirt of sanitiser just didn't cut it.

Actually going on a date was looking to be about as hard as buying toilet paper from the suddenly empty supermarket shelves.

So she did what she always did when she

needed help — she asked the girls in Bell House.

"Well, there's always online dating," Callie said. "You can get to know the guy, chatting online, before you actually meet him."

"Yeah, but there's so many ways he could fool you online," Octavia argued. "Fake profiles, fake pictures...seriously, some guys create dozens of them so they can persuade girls to send them naked pictures. And don't forget dick pics. So many guys want to send you a picture of their hairy sausage because they think you'll actually find it attractive..." She shuddered.

"There's no hurry, is there? I mean, this pandemic should be over in a few months, like the SARS and MERS scares. Or swine flu or bird flu...it'll all be a distant memory, come Christmas," Tacey said.

"It's nearly Christmas?" Rory asked, five-year-old eyes shining as only a little girl's can.

"No, sweetheart, it isn't until December. When it's summer," Tacey said. She checked her watch. "Actually, it's nearly bedtime, so you should go brush your teeth and wash your face, then put your pjs on, ready for bed."

Rory frowned, but she did as her mother said.

Alethea missed living with them all. In Bell House, there was always someone to talk to, no matter what the hour. Unlike her parents' place, where she was alone all the time. And there was talk of locking people down in their homes, like had happened in other countries, so she wouldn't even be able to visit them. Alethea shuddered. Surely the pandemic wouldn't get that bad in Australia.

"We'll help you set up your profile," Tacey said. "With Callie and Octavia here to advise you, you won't make any of the same mistakes they made."

Octavia coughed. "Mistakes Callie made, not me. I've never bothered with online dating. Online gaming, well…what else am I supposed to do in a camp in the middle of nowhere, with nothing but a decent internet connection? But this isn't about me. It's about Alethea and her quest for love. First, she'll need a good photo." She surveyed the room. "Stand here, in front of the bookcase. That'll show how much you like to read."

"What are those things on the shelf?" Alethea asked.

Everyone else laughed.

"Rory's obsessed with the Mandalorian, so she wants everything Baby Yoda. She set them all up along the bookcase so they can watch the show with her." Tacey reached for the nearest green figurine. "I'll move them out of the way."

"No! Leave them. Between the books and the figurines, it shows Alethea's into books and pop culture. Geek girls definitely get attention," Octavia said.

"But I don't even know what the green thing is," Alethea protested. "I like my aliens hot and muscled and well endowed. Not small, green and wrinkly."

"That's all right. You can mention your

passion for knobbly alien peen in your profile," Callie said.

"God, no! That'll get you triple the number of dick pics, I swear, because they think you're asking to see the goods. Do not mention penises anywhere in your profile or preferences."

"Not even if that's the only part of him you're really interested in?" Callie asked.

"Callie!" Alethea protested. "I'm supposed to be looking for love, not a hookup!"

"Well, yeah, but you have to start somewhere. A first date, your first fuck…I mean, how can you know he gives good dick unless you've sampled the goods?"

"And that is why Callie is still single, because she only dates guys who are as into first date sex as she is, which is why she never gives them a second date," Tacey said.

"Hey, good dick is an increasingly rare commodity. It's not my fault most guys don't know what to do with their dangly bits. Or any part of a woman's body, really."

"And we're back to why Alethia is looking for love, because the perfect man doesn't exist outside the pages of a book," Octavia said.

A chorus of agreement greeted that statement, which made Alethia miss living with them all the more. Sure, they bickered like siblings instead of cousins (except Octavia and Tacey, who actually were sisters), but they were family who always had each other's backs. Or dating profile, like the one Octavia had already managed to bring up on her tablet screen. Complete with a photo of Alethia in front of the bookcase that didn't look half bad.

"Right, let's get this filled out," Octavia said. "Interests?"

"Books and archaeology," Alethia said.

"Yeah, dead guys and fictional ones." Callie reached for her drink to toast Alethia's choice. "The best kind."

Tacey hushed Callie, while Octavia continued, "Favourite date activity?"

"Amazing food I don't have to cook."

They all laughed at that. Tacey was easily the

best cook among them, which was why she ran a successful café, but Alethea was hands down the worst.

"Your ideal partner?"

Alethea took a deep breath. "A history buff who likes reading and travel, who's not afraid to get his hands dirty, who's looking for a forever relationship…and gives great dick, with a gorgeous body to go with it. Oh, and he has to have a sexy voice that can take me halfway to heaven, with the skills to take me the rest of the way once the pants come off."

Callie and Tacey laughed, but Octavia was frowning at the screen. "I can put in the first bit, but the bit about getting dirty and anything after it…nope, you're going to have to word it better than that, or all you're going to get are mud wrestlers, lonely farmers and homophobes obsessed with buttsex. Not to mention an inbox full of porn." She tugged on her ear, thinking. "How about a man who's looking for the love of his life, so he can make her happy?"

Tacey raised her hand. "I'd like one of those."

More laughter, until Alethia sobered. "Yeah, that might work."

Octavia shrugged. "If it doesn't, you can just change it. I mean, your perfect match might actually be a mud wrestler or a lonely farmer. And if you do meet someone lovely who doesn't quite click, you could always introduce him to the rest of us. Callie could do the dick test, Tacey can check if he brings joy and I can do a background check, to make sure he's not some crypto king on the dark web who made all his money on drugs and sex slaves." When everyone stared at her, she just shrugged. "What? There are people out there like that, and they look like ordinary guys, not monsters at all. You have to be careful."

If Alethea hadn't resolved to do this, she probably would have given up altogether at this point, but the girls were being so helpful and hopeful…something good had to come of it, surely.

FIVE

"It's time to pay what you owe," Stan said, knowing his cousins had his back.

"But I still haven't got all of my land grant from the Governor, and my family is arriving soon. After they've settled in and the Governor gives me what he owes," whined Peel. Not Sir Thomas Peel, just plain old Mr Thomas Peel, who had long since lost any of the respect that would have earned him even an ordinary title like Mr.

"Five years we've worked for you, Peel, and now we want what we're owed. Five years of pay, and forty acres each. As promised, in the contracts we signed back in England. Everyone else left, while the four of us stood by you. Englishmen and their families went crying to the Governor to be let out of their contracts, but we're Scotsmen, and Scots always keep their word. We've done everything you asked, and these are our terms. If we can't have the acres you promised back in England, we shall have these instead." Stan held out the hand drawn map Wystan had copied from Peel's own plans. The plans the Governor had sent him, along with the grant of these lands. It might not be the entire estate Peel had been promised, but it was more than ten times the size of the paltry hundred and sixty acres Stan was asking for. "Now write a letter to the Governor, telling him you're giving us these lands under the term of our contract, for if we have to pay a visit to the Governor without that letter, we will be forced to tell him you are in breach of contract, and I've heard the prison at Van Diemen's Land is a harsh place for any man, let alone one who is accustomed to having servants. Then what will your family do when they arrive? For the Governor will surely take your lands as forfeit…"

"Enough!" Peel cried. Indeed, there appeared to be an actual tear in the corner of his eye. "You shall have your letter, and your lands. Though others might not be so honest, I, too, am a man of my word."

Less than an hour later, all four Steels piled into a boat to sail up the coast to Fremantle, where they'd take the river to Perth and the Governor's office. There, they would trade Peel's letter and the map for the titles to their own freehold land. Land they would return to, once they'd bought some supplies, enough to see them through until harvest in the summer. Maybe next year, or the year after, they'd build another cottage or three, instead of cramming into the one tiny stone cottage that had been their quarters for five years. Now, it would be home.

"And you are?" the Governor's secretary asked.

"Mr Steel," Stan said, pulling Peel's letter from his coat. "I'm here about…"

"The plans for the new mill, of course," the secretary said smoothly, rising to offer his hand to Stan. "The Governor would be delighted to lay the foundation stone."

"Uh, no, not the mill. We're here about a land grant down near the Murray River."

The secretary didn't seem to understand. "But…the mill. The Governor said you would be in today and to make sure I told you he is in favour of the new mill, just in time for the next harvest."

Stan shook his head. "I think you must have me mixed up with someone else. I'm not building a mill."

The secretary flipped feverishly through the papers on his desk. "But you are Mr William Steel, are you not?"

Stan's heart froze. William Steel was here, and not in the Americas?

He forced himself to smile. "Oh, no, William Steel is my cousin. I'm Stanley Steel." More like a second cousin, but so were Wystan, Harlow and Grant, and they were family.

"Which would make the lovely Miss Carline Steel your cousin, too, more's the pity. Quite a ravishing piece of goods, that one. I bet your cousin gets a dozen offers a day for her hand, and likely more." The secretary winked. "I bet he's holding out for an offer from one of the big landholders out at York, so he can sell her for the right price."

Carline was here, too? And likely to be sold to the highest bidder as a bride? God, did William have no shame? So much for Stan having to prove himself worthy of her. William Steel wasn't worthy to be her brother if he meant to sell her to some rich old man.

No. He could not let this happen. Not to Carline.

Stan forced out another smile. "A pity there aren't enough pretty women in the colony to be brides for us all. But time and tide wait for no man, so if you'd be so kind…we've reached an agreement with Mr Thomas Peel about some farming land along the Murray River, and we'd like to see the titles granted in our names, if you please…"

"Of course, of course."

In fairly short order, Stanley, Grant, Wystan and Harlow became landowners. They thanked the secretary and hurried out of the office.

"What's the rush?" Harlow asked.

"Didn't you hear the man? William Steel will be here shortly, and Carline is here in the colony with him, to be married off to whichever wealthy landowner he deems most worthy." Stanley waved the sheaf of papers at his cousin. "I mean to ambush him, and make sure the worthy man who wins her is me."

"Isn't he the man who struck you with his riding crop, and threatened to flog you for looking at her?" Wystan asked.

All three men stared at him in surprise.

Wystan shrugged. "What? I've lost my wife, not my wits. Unlike you, Stan, if you think the man who threatened your life for looking at his sister will let you marry her."

Perhaps Wystan was right. But he would never forgive himself if he didn't try. Five years of hard work to win this estate had to be worth something. He only hoped it would be enough to win Carline's hand.

SIX

WANT TO MEET?

Alethea just stared at the screen, her finger hovering with no idea where to land.

She'd spent three months in a love/hate relationship with the dating app Octavia had signed her up for. Which would be good if she'd felt anything akin to love for any of the guys she'd interacted with, but her feelings toward them were more like…ambivalence, bordering on boredom, which even she knew was the kiss of death in any relationship. She wanted love and passion and sparks, not…to be able to list the ten things she didn't hate about him.

The current guy asking to meet her didn't seem to be the sort of crazy crypto kingpin Octavia had warned her about. He worked at some mine site up north, posting pictures of the desert landscape and skies every few days when he was on site. He had a good eye for colour and he knew a fair bit about birds, or at least the ones he took pictures of. He sounded nice.

But she wasn't looking for nice. She was looking for love, with a side order of seriously hot sex.

Her gut instinct said to tell him no. To hold out for something more.

But she was sick of being alone in her parents' apartment, only leaving to pick up takeaway food from one of the few restaurants that managed to remain open through all the restrictions. With the restrictions easing next week, and restaurants actually allowed to serve people at tables again, just the thought of being able to share a meal with someone, anyone, whether he was a nice guy or some crazy crypto kingpin…

He'd at least have interesting dinner conversation that she hadn't heard a hundred times before, right?

SURE, she found herself typing. She began to him when and where, then reconsidered. If this was to be her first time eating out in months, she wanted to know it would be good, so she named a restaurant not far from her parents' house, and asked him when he'd be available.

The answer came back immediately:

FRIDAY NEXT WEEK AT 7?

A little over a week away. Well, at least she'd be able to tell Mum she'd finally gone on a date, Alethea thought as she typed her acceptance. She'd head out, have a nice meal, maybe some nice conversation, and slowly work up the courage to ask him if he gave good dick. How bad could it be?

SEVEN

The tide left without them, for Stan was too busy drowning his sorrows in drink to heed his cousins' call to come with them, and they were not so callous as to leave without him.

"I told you he would not allow you to marry her," Wystan said, shaking his head.

"It's not just that," Stan seethed. "It's that he dares to call me unworthy, when he's no better than any of us! Someone should teach him a lesson."

"I heard tell the natives already have. They stole all the flour in his mill not long ago," Grant said. "Maybe we should do the same."

Harlow slammed his hands on the table. "NO! Listen to yourselves. We're not thieves. We have coin enough to buy the flour we need."

"It's not about what we need. It's about what Stan needs," Grant said. "You heard William say himself that he'll be headed to Fremantle next, so he won't be home tonight. We could sneak in, under the cover of darkness, and leave with no one the wiser, and enough flour to see us to harvest."

"It's not flour or vengeance I want, but Carline," Stan protested. He lifted his tankard to his lips, and a brilliant idea struck him. He dropped the tankard down on the table again. "We're true Scots, are we not?"

"YES!"

"Of course."

"Yes…"

"And stealing brides is an ancient Scottish custom…" he continued.

"No," Harlow began, but Stan wouldn't be silenced.

"Tonight, we'll go to the mill, and kidnap Carline. We'll take her down to our farm, where we'll keep her safe from her brother and all her rich suitors, until she sees the light and agrees to marry me," Stan finished proudly.

"And steal all his flour while we're at it," Grant finished. "It's brilliant!"

"It's stupid," Harlow snapped.

"It is traditional, and if he truly loves her…" Wystan looked wistful. Likely thinking of his own dead wife.

It took another hour or two to convince them all, and Harlow maintained he was only going along to make sure they didn't get into trouble, but by then Stan already had a plan. He only prayed that nothing would go wrong.

EIGHT

Alethia couldn't remember doing this much preparation for a date since the Year 12 ball, and she hadn't even had a date for that one.

Then again, she hadn't had to consider having sex with anyone after the ball, while tonight, if he was even halfway decent, she would seriously consider it. So she'd gone out and bought new matching lacy lingerie, but she'd hidden it under a demure knee length dress and stockings. While she'd been in the adult shop buying the stockings (because sex shops sold the best stockings, she'd learned from a friend who did competitive dancing), she'd also splashed out on a box of the really good condoms, as well as a novelty one to give to Octavia on her birthday, because that's what you gave Octavia for her birthday. She couldn't remember how long ago the tradition started, but what mattered was that she kept it going, so she did.

While she was paying for her purchases, the girl behind the counter asked, "Have you seen our new vibrators? It's the top selling model in the US market and it comes in five colours." She waved her hand across the display of deluxe dick-shaped devices, wiggling her fingers like she was working magic.

Alethea considered them. The devices were probably better than most men, and likely the yardstick Callie would compare a real man to, in order to determine whether he gave good dick. Hell, if she didn't get lucky on this date, with even passable dick or whatever other part of his body he knew how to pleasure her with, she'd probably need one of these.

But she didn't want a machine. She wanted a man. That's why she'd made this crazy new year's resolution in the first place, and being stuck at home alone in her parents' place during a pandemic had just made her realise how much she wanted to connect with someone. Mentally as well as physically. More than anything, Alethia didn't want to be alone any more.

But if she bought one now, that would be admitting defeat, before she'd even gone into battle. Well, it was love, not war, but surely the principles were the same.

"No, thank you," Alethea said firmly.

"Are you sure? I only unpacked them this morning, and they're whizzing out the door like you wouldn't believe. We'll probably be sold out by Monday, and who knows when the next shipment will arrive, what with all the passenger planes grounded and all." She winked. "I promise you'll regret it if you don't get one now."

Maybe, but she'd lived twenty-four years without owning a vibrator, and none of her cousins had one. Hell, no one she knew owned one, even if they did appear in books a lot. Maybe it was an American thing, because American guys didn't know how to do it, so girls over there had to take matters into their own hands.

Aussie girls were different, and, hopefully, at least one Aussie guy would be, too.

She finished her outfit off with a pair of ankle boots with high heels. Just in case he was tall, so it'd be easier for him to kiss her. Or for her to kiss him…

Now, the important decision: should she wear her hair up or down? She'd had it up in her profile picture, and she usually braided it back for work, but guys liked long hair and hers was nearly down to her waist. Of course, being braided all day, it would be wavy if she didn't take a straightener to it, which would take at least an hour, maybe two, which she didn't really have time for right now. So she brushed it back into a high ponytail, and hoped that would be enough.

If it wasn't…maybe there'd still be a vibrator left for her to buy on Monday.

NINE

They hid in the bushes, overlooking the millpond, while they waited for William Steel to leave. He seemed to take forever loading up the flour sacks. Grant grumbled that there would be none left for them to steal, and Harlow hushed him before Stan could say anything. At least two of them had their heads on straight. Wystan seemed to have retreated in his own little world again, daydreaming about what he might do if his wife were still alive, no doubt.

Finally, William loaded up the last sack and climbed aboard the boat himself. Stan almost cheered aloud as they steamed downriver.

"Now?" Grant asked, his eyes shining with eagerness.

"No, you idiot. We wait until sundown," Harlow snapped.

The sun was an especially slow snail tonight, of all nights, when everything Stan wanted was so close he could almost grasp it.

"All right, just like we agreed. We three see what is in the mill, while you, Stan, go steal yourself a bride," Harlow said grimly.

Stan nodded, then darted away, keeping low so as not to be seen, as he rounded the campsite. The grey canvas tent drooped in the moonlight, as if it, too, was miserable that Carline was forced to live in such squalor. Why, the stone cottage he and his cousins had built on the land that Peel had given them was far superior to this…he could not even call it a hovel, for to do so would be an insult to the sturdiness of such a structure.

The tent looked like one gust of winter wind would blow it over. Perhaps that was why William meant to sell her to some York farmer – so that she might not spend another night beneath canvas. Perhaps he did care for her welfare, after all.

But he could not care for her anywhere near as much as Stan did, and Stan would give her everything her heart desired, if it was to be found in the colony.

He crept up to the tent, then slipped inside, searching for Carline's bed. He found beds, all right, but both of them were empty.

She wasn't here. That meant she must be in the mill.

The mill his cousins meant to plunder…

Stan broke into a run.

A gunshot echoed through the bush, followed by two more. He thought he heard Grant's voice, but he could not discern the words.

Stan ran faster. He did not know how Grant had gotten his hands on the weapon, but he was as reckless a shooter as he was about everything else. What if he accidentally shot Carline? Stan would never forgive himself if she got hurt.

He rounded the mill, staying close to the shadows that hugged its walls as he searched for the door. Locked, thank goodness – if she was hiding inside, she was safe.

He put his shoulder to the door, heaving against it with all his weight, but the wood didn't budge. Australian hardwood was a match for the most solid oak at home.

A rustling sound above made him look up. A flash of silvery white, nay, silver, before…

BOOM.

Pain blasted his shoulder, setting his whole arm on fire.

Stan dropped to his knees, before he pitched forward, unconscious before his face hit her threshold.

TEN

Alethea arrived fifteen minutes early, unable to wait at home any longer without chewing her lipstick off. Only to realise she then had to decide whether she wanted wine or not while she waited. Damn it, she wanted to ask the girls what she should do, but it'd took bad if he arrived and she was staring at her phone.

Wine would relax her, but what if he was late and she finished it, so she had to order another glass? She didn't want to end up drunk by the end of the date. Besides, it usually worked out better to order a bottle to share than buy wine by the glass, but what if he didn't drink? Or what if he didn't drink wine?

So she drummed her fingers on the table as she drank her glass of water and waited.

She shouldn't have come. She wanted to go home. She should just order takeaway food and leave…

Did she want to die alone, with only a vibrator for company?

Alethea could almost hear Tacey's voice telling her off.

Tacey was right, of course. Alethea was here because she wanted to find love, like in the books she read. So many books while she'd been stuck in that apartment alone.

"Excuse me, I'm here to have dinner with my soul mate? Well, we haven't actually met yet, but I knew she was my soul mate the moment I saw her profile picture. We're going to have babies together and I'm going to stay home to take care of them, and homeschool them so I can teach them everything I know."

Someone at the table next to her began to laugh, covering it up with her hand. She wasn't the only one, either – everyone seemed to be staring at the guy who was telling the maître d' his future plans.

Then he turned to face the restaurant and…it was HIM.

"Alethea!"

He'd grown a beard. His hair looked like it hadn't been washed in weeks. He was wearing a t-shirt with that hideous green wrinkly alien Rory loved on the front. And, worst of all, he had a thin, reedy voice that set her teeth on edge.

She could excuse almost anything – the beard, the hair, the shirt – but that voice…she wasn't going to be able to listen to a word he said without wincing. Without a sexy voice, there was no way he was getting anywhere near her bed tonight. Or ever.

Her phone beeped, and she whipped it out.

A message from Octavia: ENJOY YOUR HOT DATE TONIGHT. CALL WITH DETAILS TOMORROW.

Alethea felt sick. There was no way she was going to be able to go through with this.

Yet here he was, about to take the seat in front of her.

"Hi," he said breathlessly, staring at her like a parched man about to drink her up.

Bile rose up in her throat. "Really sorry, but work just sent me a message. They need me for something urgent. Have to go. Sorry." She jumped out of her seat and practically ran for the door.

Nope nope nope nope nope…all the way home.

ELEVEN

Stan woke up choking, no, drowning, just like that time Grant had thought it was a good idea to teach him to swim by tossing him over the side of the boat. Water filled his mouth, his throat, blocking out all air...

But the pain in his shoulder was gone. Stan relaxed, no longer fighting the liquid so that it could flow down the proper channels to where it would do him good instead of harm.

"Good boy," a feminine voice purred.

So that was what her voice sounded like, for it could belong to no one other than Carline. Who was now dressing his wounds, whatever they were. Her hands were unbelievably soft as she stroked his chest. Putting some healing salve on him, perhaps? Must be. He'd heard silly tales, back in Scotland, about her being a witch, but he'd known they were lies. Perhaps she had some skill with herbs, as was expected of the lady of the house, and she could practice her herbcraft on him for as long as she liked.

A stab of pain bit into his chest, right between his ribs. God, but it hurt. Like being stabbed in the heart, which could not be, for he was still living, breathing.

"Carline…what…what are you doing?"

That was William Steel's voice, shaking in a manner Stan had never heard before. A wild sort of satisfaction came over him. If Carline could frighten her brother so, then it was a good thing.

Another stab to his heart, followed by a

third cut, deeper than the first two. It was all Stan could do not to scream.

"It's not what you think, William. These men attacked the mill. I had no choice but to shoot them. They were armed with axes, look."

Stan wanted to sit up so he might look, too. How dare anyone attack Carline? He'd come here to protect her. To protect her always. From mad axe men and her mercenary brother and any other man who dared to even look at her with lust in his eyes. She was his to protect!

"Help me dig graves for them, William. Around the walls of the mill."

What a strange place for graves. Didn't dead men belong in the burial ground, just outside Perth? Or the one in Fremantle. Then again, not everyone could be buried so close to town. Peel's ill-fated settlers who died on the beach in Clarence had been laid to rest not far from their squalid tents. Stan and several other strong men had been asked to dig graves in the sand dunes behind the camp, to bury the bodies. He suspected that's why Peel had headed south, instead of building a proper town in Clarence, like he'd originally planned. Didn't want to be haunted by the ghosts of the families who'd died, believing in the promises he'd never fulfilled.

"What have you done?" William hissed. "This is Grant Steel, our cousin."

The axe men had killed Grant? Oh, no. Poor Grant. So full of life. Stan couldn't bear the thought that his cousin was dead.

"And that's Stanley Steel, another cousin! Carline, you've killed family!"

No she hadn't! He was still alive, Stan wanted to shout, but he couldn't seem to move. The strangest lassitude spread through his body, like he'd drunk a bottle of the finest whisky and it was flowing all the way down to his toes.

Except whisky would have burned and this felt cold. Cold and dark. Almost like death.

Stan tried to shout a protest, but he was too late. The darkness had him now.

TWELVE

The next morning, Alethea deleted the dating app off her phone, before spending the whole weekend writing the literature review for her thesis. When her cousins texted her to ask about the date, she just told them it was a waste of time.

Monday morning, it was all hands on deck at the dig site, and the week went by in a whirlwind of work, punctuated by quick trips to the supermarket or one of the nearby lunch bars. On Friday, she decided to go back to the same restaurant as her disastrous date, just to pick up takeaway. For a moment, she thought she spotted him, before a family trooped through to their table, blocking her view. When the family were seated, the guy was gone.

She must have imagined him, Alethea told herself, as she paid for her order, thanked the server, and left.

That might have been the first time, but it certainly wasn't the last. She began to see him everywhere – at the supermarket, at the lunchbars, even outside the cemetery, but every time she tried to get a closer look, he vanished, or it turned out not to be him.

Like the cemetery didn't have enough ghosts haunting the place, she'd had to invent a new one.

"Are you all right?" her boss, Jeremy, asked. "You just seem…jumpy. You didn't believe the security guard's story, did you?"

"What story?" She must have missed it.

"This morning when we got in, I caught him telling some of the staff that he'd seen a kilted Scotsman playing the bagpipes every night this week, only when he went up to him to tell him he wasn't allowed on the property, the Scotsman vanished into thin air. He's making it up, I'm certain of it."

Alethea managed a watery smile. So she wasn't the only one seeing ghosts. "No, I'm not worried about some piper in a kilt. I've never seen him, and seeing as I'm staying only a couple of streets away, I'd have heard the bagpipes from my place. Well, unless it was last night, and then all I heard was the couple from downstairs having a screaming match over whose turn it was to take out the rubbish. I'm surprised neither of them ended up in one of the rubbish bins this morning."

"God, if the neighbours are that bad, you should move."

Alethea shrugged. "I'm housesitting for my parents, while they're overseas, so I can't.

Besides, they don't argue every night. Just bin night. It's free, and walking distance to work. I used to live in a share house with a few of my cousins. They were way noisier, and I guess I kind of got used to it."

She should probably call them, if only to tell them what had actually happened on her date. She'd been getting increasingly curious messages from the girls all week.

On the weekend, she promised herself. There was too much work to do before then.

THIRTEEN

When Friday finally rolled around again, Alethea was exhausted. She'd worked some full-on digs in the past, but never ones that lasted this long. They'd been excavating for months, and they still had half the site to cover.

"We've got another empty one here!" someone called.

"Another one? That's three empty graves

this week," Jeremy grumbled. He'd been working alongside them all week, instead of staying in the office and talking to clients. There must be some pressure on him to get this job finished. "If I didn't know better, I'd wonder if there was something in the ground that made them get up and walk off. Like something out of a zombie movie. Or vampires, maybe."

"Zombies and vampires don't exist any more than ghosts do," Alethea said. "Or aliens." More's the pity, because the ones in her books were way hotter than any human male she'd ever met.

"So you don't believe in the Fremantle zombie? Or the Moth Man?"

"I know for a fact those viral Moth Man videos were filmed by a media student at my cousin's café. Total hoax." Tacey would kill her for saying so, but it wasn't like Jeremy was going to go to Tacey's café for a coffee with a side order of monster hunting.

"And the zombie?"

She shrugged. "I never heard about a zombie."

"It was before the Moth Man. Someone dug up a grave under the art college oval in Fremantle. Probably just a high school prank, but the newspaper article said the grave was empty. Like the body just got up and walked away."

"There's a graveyard under a school oval? Seriously?"

"Well, this one was under a school tennis court. Would it surprise you?"

Alethia had to admit that it wouldn't. "Yeah, but…ugh. They should have moved the bodies, like we're doing here."

"Just as long as we don't find any zombies, it's all good." Jeremy clambered to his feet. "I'm getting a coffee. You want one?"

She considered for a moment, then said, "No, I want to finish this one before lunch."

Now he was gone, she could listen to her audiobook again. The day went quicker that way. She flicked it from pause to play and resumed working.

The coffin fragments appeared first beneath her brush, slivers of wood that had been smashed into a million pieces by time and the weight of the bitumen that had sat on top of it for so long. She paused to take some pictures for the record, before she began picking up the pieces and putting them in a box.

Then she heard the clink of metal. Oh, there was a coffin plaque, perfect. This grave had belonged to Mary Craig, who was….Alethea took a moment to subtract the dates. Mary had only been eight years old when she died, poor thing. Which meant she had to be very careful with this grave, because the bones would be smaller and more delicate than most of the adult ones. If there were bones left at all.

More photos, before she carefully lifted the coffin plaque into the box and began to brush at the soil again. Wait, there was something white. It could be…

Alethea screamed and leaped back.

Jeremy came racing over. "What is it?"

"It's…the eyes opened…" Alethea gasped out.

Everyone converged on her, peering into the grave to see for themselves. Yes, there was a girl's face there, staring up at them with eerie blue eyes. Like some kind of…

"It's a doll. A porcelain doll," someone breathed.

A doll? Just a doll? Alethia almost laughed with relief. And here she thought she'd been staring into Mary Craig's eyes, instead of the girl's doll.

An hour's careful work with her brushes and everyone could see the truth – that little Mary Craig's parents had buried her with her doll. A very lifelike doll that had nearly given Alethia a heart attack.

"You should probably knock off early today. Take the afternoon off," Alethia heard Jeremy say. "Let someone else finish up this grave."

Numbly, she nodded. She tugged off her gloves and headed for the temporary site office, where she could store her gear before heading home.

"Alethia, wait!"

She paused and turned.

"I need to talk to you. I'm certain we're soul mates, destined to have children together."

Children. Oh God, she didn't want anything to do with children at all right now. Just the image of those blue eyes opening…

Alethia shook her head and broke into a run. She didn't stop until she'd locked the apartment door behind her, when she put her back to the wall and slid down until her butt hit the floor.

Only then did she realise she'd not only seen him, but heard him. Outside her workplace, of all places. Which meant he knew where she worked, and if he'd followed her, he probably now knew where she lived, too, if he hadn't known that already.

Wonderful. First undead children, and now she had a stalker.

Her life was such a fucking mess right now.

FOURTEEN

"Alethea? Oh, hey!"

Just hearing Tacey's voice made her feel a bit better about everything.

"One sec, I'll put you on speaker so I don't have to repeat everything for Callie."

Too bad if Alethea wanted to talk to Tacey privately. Not that she could remember the last time she'd done that. There were no secrets in Bell House. Well, not from the other girls who lived there, anyway, even if they did keep secrets from the rest of the world outside.

"Right. Callie's just getting a drink, but she wants to know how many condoms you used on your date the other night, and whether you remembered to get the good ones."

Alethea closed her eyes. Yep, that was Callie all right. "I didn't use any. I still have a full box."

"What? He was that good you want to have his babies?" Callie shrieked from somewhere in the background.

"No. There was no sex, safe or otherwise. I left early."

"Oh shit. What'd he do?" Tacey asked. "Tell me the dinner was good, at least."

Alethia swallowed. "I left before we ordered."

"Did he smell bad?"

"Was he a jerk?"

Alethia sighed. "He sounded like Justin Bieber."

Hysterical laughter came down the line.

Tacey recovered first. "You know, there are probably a lot of girls out there who'd find that attractive."

"Yeah, but she wants a guy with a voice like a phone sex operator. All deep and growly and…what was it you said when Octavia was here? That he had to have a voice that could get you halfway to heaven? More like so devilishly sexy he could persuade you to be his mistress in hell!" Callie dissolved into laughter again.

"So what if I have a thing for dark, sexy voices? It's the one thing I won't compromise on. The problem with this guy wasn't just his voice, though. It was what he was saying."

"What did he say?" Tacey asked.

"He said I was his soul mate and he was talking about having kids." Like poor little Mary Craig.

"Well, that's…not so bad, I guess. At least he's not afraid of commitment." Tacey didn't sound like she believed it, though.

"Not so bad if I was interested, but I left.

Now I see him everywhere I go. He even showed up outside the dig site where I work!"

"Wait…now Justin Bieber is stalking you? I am so going to curse him!" Callie said.

"He's not Justin Bieber. He just sort of sounds like him. And you can't curse him." Mostly because curses didn't actually exist, no matter how many times Callie threatened people with them. Oh, she had a collection of old books on witchcraft that said how to cast curses, but Callie was usually the first person to admit magic didn't exist. Well, except when she was threatening to curse some guy, of course.

"If it scares off your stalker, you bet I can. All I have to do is make him believe I can, and he'll run far and fast. Remember that possessive guy I dated once, who thought we were forever when he was so just a one night stand? He believed I'd given him a horrible, incurable rash."

"Was that the one where you put cayenne pepper in his underpants?" Tacey asked.

"A good witch never reveals her ingredients, but that might have been one of them," Callie said loftily.

"More like the only ingredient," Tacey muttered.

"Hey, you can't talk. Business is booming at your café because of a hoax Moth Man that's been making my work life hell! Do you know how many theology professors believe your creature not only exists, but is some hitherto undiscovered kind of demon, and if they can only write enough papers on it, they'll have enough funding to see them into retirement?"

Even Tacey and Callie bickering helped lift Alethia's spirits. "I wish you girls were here."

"Well, we should be. I know! Next girls' night, we can all come to your place. Let's see…Mum wants to have Rory over for a sleepover in a couple of weeks, and Octavia will be back then, too."

"Where is Octavia?" Alethia asked.

"Doing a fly-in-fly-out IT support job up north at some mine site. She left this morning.

As soon as she's back, we'll descend on your place, and between the four of us, we'll find a way to scare your stalker off for good, okay?"

"Okay." Alethia could hardly refuse. Besides, it had been ages since they'd had a girls' night, what with the restrictions and all. She just had to hang on until then.

FIFTEEN

When the girls arrived at Alethea's apartment, she couldn't help but stand in the doorway, staring. "Are we going dancing?" she asked, confused. Cafés and restaurants might be open, but nightclubs weren't.

Tacey rolled her eyes. "Oh, I'm going to let Callie explain this one. Especially as you'll have to dress up, too. I haven't worn these pants since before Rory was born. I'm surprised they still fit."

"I'm not," Octavia said, pushing past her sister to enter the apartment. "You spent all your time cooking in the café, so most days you forget to eat. After eating camp food for the last few weeks, I'm surprised I haven't gone up a size." She tossed her hair, and Alethea realised she'd changed the colour again – now it had iridescent green streaks slicing through the inky black.

"Yeah, yeah, you're both turning into whales," Callie said. "Next thing you know, the fridge will be full of krill." She winked at Alethia as she sidled inside. "You should probably get changed, by the way. Think warm, but dark and sexy."

Warm, dark and sexy was what she'd wanted, and gotten a stalker instead, Alethia grumbled to herself as she closed the door behind Tacey.

The girls arranged themselves around the lounge room while Alethia dug through her clothes for something suitable. She didn't have leather pants like Octavia or Tacey, or ones with more cutouts than cloth, like Callie's, but she did have a pair of tight black jeans that laced up the sides. She paired it with a see-through silvery top over a lacy black bra that practically begged to be seen.

When Alethea returned to the lounge, Callie raised a glass to her. "Now if you don't look like the perfect package of demon bait, I'll offer myself up instead."

"Wait…what?" Alethea stammered. She couldn't be serious.

"Tell her, Callie," Tacey said tiredly. She handed Alethea a glass. "Have a drink first. You'll need it."

Alethea took a gulp, then nearly choked. That had to be straight vodka, and a strong one, at that. "What's wrong with mixers?" she rasped.

Callie giggled. "You evidently haven't been buying much at the liquor store lately. There are limits on how much you can buy. One carton or two bottles. And no self respecting demon is going to come near a passionfruit premix, so I got the vodka. I want this to have the best chance to work, you see…"

Tacey waved her hand, indicating for Callie to continue.

"Okay. I found a spell book which may or may not be the genuine article. I have it on good authority that one of the spells may have actually worked and if there's any time to test it, it's when we actually need the help. The plan is to summon you a demon protector, who will stick around to scare off your stalker for as long as you need him, and then you just send him back to hell. The demon, I mean."

Alethea opened her mouth to object. This was a terrible idea.

But Callie pulled out a sheaf of papers from her coat pocket and began to pass them out. "I've translated the spell as best I could and printed out copies for all of us. Traditionally, it's done by one really powerful witch, but it also says in the book that a coven of four or more women — yes, it definitely says women and not witches – will have the combined power to perform spells, with the right ingredients." She set a small cooler box on the coffee table. "Now, traditionally, the ritual is done skyclad, which means naked, but I figure seeing as it's winter and we're trying to summon a demon, dressing sexy and showing a bit of skin should be enough."

Tacey set her empty glass on the coffee table, beside the cooler. "I still find it hard to believe you found a spell that worked. You're always the first person to say magic doesn't exist."

Callie blew out a breath. "I know. Magic doesn't exist, or I didn't think it did, but I was talking to someone recently who led me to believe it might. Maybe."

Tacey's eyes narrowed. "Is that what you were talking to Ben about? Seriously, Callie, he's a fantasy artist. He mostly does portraits while he's the artist in residence at the café, but I commissioned him to do a series of cartoons where the Moth Man comes in for coffee or muffins or…he even had him doing the dishes in one, because he'd forgotten his wallet and that was the only way he could pay for his coffee." She shook her head. "If he drew you a demon, he made it up. Much like the Moth Man, demons don't exist. Ask Rochelle. She'll show you the unedited video."

The Shut Up Café had an artist in residence? Wow, Alethea missed all the fun stuff. "I should come down to the café, and see if he can draw me as an elf or a dragon or something."

"He only works evenings, but, sure, come in whenever you like. I should warn you, he has a thing for Rochelle, though, so he's kind of already taken," Tacey said.

Callie laughed. "Pity, because that guy's got to be the epitome of good dick, if you see Rochelle in the mornings. You can tell when she's spent a night with him, because she's practically glowing with best-sex-ever vibes in the morning." When she found the other girls staring at her she shrugged. "What? At least someone's getting some."

Alethea looked down at the printed page in her hands. "We're supposed to find consecrated ground, under the light of the moon, then place a heart still moist with the blood of our kin in a circle of salt and candles and runes, then say the right words to summon the demon, who will then consume the heart. Um, there is absolutely no way I'm going to let you kill someone to cast a spell that probably won't work just to scare off my stalker!"

Callie grinned. "Relax, I didn't have to kill anyone for it. One of the lab techs in the School of Medicine owed me a favour, so I figured it was time to call it in." She opened the cooler with a flourish.

Oh, ew.

"Callie, you didn't!"

"Is that really a…?"

"It's a pig's heart. The first years dissect them, and the abattoir sends them by the bucketload. The rest of the pig's probably already been turned into sausages and steaks, so it's not like we have to dispose of a body or anything."

Alethea wasn't sure how much of an improvement that was. It was bigger than her fist and all covered in blood…

"Yeah, but not even a demon's going to believe that pig was a member of your family," Octavia said.

Callie winced. "Uh, yeah, there's no getting around that part. So, I brought some micro lancets – sterile ones – so we can each prick a finger and drip a couple of drops of blood each on the heart. We're all family, so that's the kinsblood sorted, and no one has to die." She looked around. "Come on, one quick prick and it's done. Best if we do it here, so we can wash up and put bandaids on and stuff, because there's still the salt, and I have a bottle of pig's blood for the runes. We just need to find consecrated ground. I was thinking maybe outside the cathedral…"

"The cemetery. It's all consecrated ground, with a church and everything," Alethea said.

Callie grinned. "That's the spirit! How far away is it?"

"Only a little way down the road, but the main cemetery is all fenced off, and the gates are locked. We'd be better off at the dig site. It's still part of the cemetery, but I know the security code for the key, and the ground is already cleared, so it'd be a lot easier to do on bare sand, and just brush away the evidence afterward." Oh hell, she was going to go through with this, wasn't she? If she was already planning it…

"If we're going to do this, I vote we get dinner afterwards, because there's no way I'm going to be able to keep anything down if you expect me to paint with actual blood," Tacey said.

The others agreed, so Callie held up her hands. "All right, so here's the plan. We go out to the graveyard, perform the summoning ritual, give the demon time to get here if he's coming, and if he's not…well, we'll know for sure that magic and demons don't exist, and we can come back here and pig out on pizza and finish off the rest of the vodka, while we watch Sam and Dean hunt monsters and stuff, because watching Jensen Ackles' butt always puts me in a better mood."

"And if Alethea's stalker turns up?" Octavia asked.

Callie's grin was decidedly dark. "Then we threaten to make him part of the ritual, and scare the shit out of him."

Alethea grabbed the bottle and took a big swig of vodka. Maybe if she drank enough, she might be able to convince herself that this was a good idea.

SIXTEEN

Alethea directed them to a spot where they'd already finished excavating, beside the spoil heap where they could leave the debris from their silly ritual and no one would be the wiser, come Monday morning. Maybe they'd be really lucky and it would rain over the weekend, washing all the evidence away. They'd have to bury the heart, though, because leaving body parts around a cemetery just wasn't right.

The whole thing looked like a big, mystical bullseye, or it would have, if you were flying above it. Did demons fly? She'd seen pictures of them with and without wings, and Callie hadn't said what sort of demon they were supposed to be summoning. The protective kind, supposedly, but that made no sense, because in all the stories she'd ever heard, demons were definitely bad.

Maybe if she just told her stalker to go away enough times, he'd leave her alone. Forget all of this soul mate nonsense. Not to mention babies…

Alethia shuddered. She'd helped out with Rory on occasion, but she had no desire to be a young mum like Tacey. In five or ten years, maybe. If it was a choice between pregnancy and putting her PhD on hold, or summoning demons…she'd pick demons, every time. Mostly because demons didn't exist and there'd be pizza with the girls afterwards, of course, but…

"Right. Now we need to say the incantation.

You have to be really explicit. Like: Demon, we summon you to enter this circle, so that you will help protect us. The original incantation was all singular – I command you to protect me – but as we're all doing this, we need the unity. The words aren't as important as the intention, and you have to be firm. Because if you summon and don't have control over it…bad things happen."

They must be bad for Callie not to describe them in gory detail. But demons didn't exist, so nothing bad would happen. At least, that's what Alethea told herself.

"Okay, now we should all stand around the circle, holding hands, and keep repeating the incantation until something happens," Callie said.

Callie's hand was hot and clammy, but Octavia's was icy cold. Across the circle, Tacey looked determined. If a demon did turn up and threaten them, Alethea didn't like its chances against Tacey. No one hurt her family.

"We summon you, demon…"

"…enter the circle…"

"…help protect us…"

"We summon you!"

"…help protect us…"

Round and round it went, voices blending into a blur of sound, like one of those round robin song things you did at primary school. Only this wasn't about some kookaburra laughing in a tree. This was dark and serious and some sort of power was humming between their joined hands, in the circle. Alethea could feel it, thrumming through her bones. She wanted to stop, but she couldn't. Had to keep chanting. Had to finish this, whatever it was, because if they didn't do this spell right, there was no telling what would happen.

Was that the flutter of wings she heard? Big wings, like the bats up in Broome?

No, it was just the dust barrier on the fence, flapping in the night breeze, surely.

Then the telltale beeps of someone opening the lockbox with the keys inside.

Alethea let go of her friends' hands. "That's the security guard. Quick, make all this disappear, while I think of something to tell him."

The candles went back into the box, still smoking slightly, as Alethea kicked sand over the salt and blood.

Oh shit, the heart…

Alethea and Callie went for it at the same time, only Alethea tripped over Callie's leg and went down. She felt something go the wrong way and then, a moment later, pain screamed through her foot.

By the time she could see again, the heart was gone, and Callie was dusting her hands off.

"Right, let's go," Tacey said. "Over the fence, before the security guy comes in."

"Can't," Alethea said. "I've twisted my ankle."

"What do we do?" Callie asked.

"You three go over the fence, and I'll distract him, by asking for help. I'm the only one who's actually authorised to be here.

I'll…tell him I forgot something, and came back to get it, then tripped and twisted my ankle in the dark. He'll have to help me, which will give you time to get to…ah, I only have one key, and I can't give it to you, or that'll look suspicious. Um…go to the car. I'll text you when I get home safe." The gate was already swinging open. "GO!"

The others sprinted off into the darkness, while Alethea could only groan. The slightest movement hurt like hell. This was worse than the time she'd twisted her ankle in hockey at school, and had to be carried off the field.

"Help," Alethea said, her voice scratchy from all the chanting. Stupid spell. She cleared her throat. "Someone, please help me. I've fallen and twisted my ankle and I need help!"

"I'll help you, miss."

The most amazing voice, so deep and dark and dipped in a distinct Scottish accent…it turned her insides liquid. If the dating app guy had sounded like this…her vocabulary would have been reduced to one, breathy word.

"Yes."

Warm arms closed around her, lifting her up, and Alethea sighed in relief.

SEVENTEEN

HELP.

One word echoed through Stanley's head like it was a bell.

Must protect her.

He fought his way through a tangle of bodies, clawing for the surface. Yet when he rose into the air, he was not alone.

Demons. Huge, horned, winged demons, flying shoulder to shoulder with him like soldiers marching into battle. Brothers in arms.

Until he saw her.

A flash of silvery blonde hair, spread out on the ground, for she'd fallen.

HELP.

The voice was hers.

"Mine," he growled, swooping in to claim her.

EIGHTEEN

Pain greyed Alethia's vision, but it didn't dull her hearing. The dust barriers were beating in the wind again, just like wings, and the chill night breeze stroked her face, keeping her conscious, but just barely. She probably shouldn't have had so much vodka, but how else was she supposed to stay warm in winter when she was only wearing a skimpy top? And pants, of course. Couldn't go to a graveyard without pants. Imagine all the corpses, looking up your skirt as you went by. They'd get an eyeful.

Like that blue-eyed doll that had scared her silly. Bile rose up in her throat at the memory.

"Wait, stop, I'm going to be sick," she mumbled to the man carrying her. "Put me down, quick!"

He set her down on her feet, but her ankle wouldn't hold her, sending a stab of pain all the way up her leg as she fell to her knees.

Never drinking vodka again, she thought to herself as she threw up most of it at the poor man's feet.

Wait…why were they on concrete? How did they get to be on…a rooftop?

"Need to get down. Need to get home," she said to his feet. And they were his feet, not his shoes. What kind of security guard went to work without shoes?

She let her gaze drift upward.

Or…pants…or any clothes at all…and were those…wings?

Now she knew she'd drunk too much vodka. Because the spell couldn't possibly have worked. She couldn't possibly be looking up at the impressive package of her own, personal demon protector.

"Who the fuck are you?"

"I am your demon protector, at your command, miss," he said in That Voice.

"Get me up off the ground, er, roof, please, demon protector," she said.

In a moment, she was in his arms again. Up against a rock hard chest with muscles all the way down and wings. He really had wings.

"Take me home, please," she said.

"Where is your home, miss?"

Oh, God, she wanted him to use that voice in her ear, while he did very bad things to her. And maybe some good things, too. All kinds of things.

Probably best to do them at home, though. Not on some random rooftop.

"Where is your home, miss?" he said again.

Demons weren't known for their patience.

She needed to gather her wits, and fast. She peered down. "Uh, that's my balcony, over there." She pointed.

In a few wingbeats, Mr Hot and Hard with Horns set them both down on her parents' balcony, narrowly missing the wrought iron lace table and chairs. Only the door to go inside wouldn't open. Locked.

"Oh, wait, I have the keys for this one." She fumbled in her pocket for them, then fumbled with the lock for even longer.

The demon sighed. He set her down on one of the chairs, picked up the keys she'd dropped between two delicate claws, and had the door open a moment later.

Then she was in his arms again. How he managed to fit those huge wings through the sliding door, she didn't know, but somehow he did it, for he stood in her parents' lounge room, towering over the furniture.

"Shall I set you down now, miss?"

No. Never.

She really hoped she hadn't said that out

loud.

God, it was hard to think. Between the hot demon and the vodka still sloshing around in her brain and how much her ankle hurt…

Hurt. There were pills for that.

"Take me to the bathroom."

He bent down so that she could grab some pain relief from the cabinet, and a cup of water to wash it down with. Then three more, to chase away the bile and make sure she wouldn't have a hangover. That done, there was only one place she wanted to go.

"Take me to bed, please, demon protector."

And he did.

NINETEEN

Stan set her on the bed. She lay still for a moment, before she started thrashing about, like a fresh-caught fish. Too late he realised she was trying to unfasten her scandalously small shirt.

"I'll go make you some tea," he mumbled, rushing out of the room.

He knew he'd found the kitchen, because there were plates and cups in a sink, and more in the cupboards above it, but it wasn't like any kitchen he'd ever seen before. In order to boil water, he needed to fire up the stove, but beneath the hotplates was only a cupboard full of pots – no space to light a fire at all. Nor was there wood or coal to burn.

There was a kettle, but it sat on the bench, tethered to the wall, beside a tea tin that contained paper pouches, instead of tea leaves.

He couldn't make tea.

But he had to make tea for Carline, because that was the civilised thing to do, and if he didn't do the right thing, she might not agree to be his bride and that's why he'd stolen her…

He would simply have to go to her and admit he did not know how to make tea in her strange kitchen. Surely she would give him some credit for wanting to do the right thing?

He trudged back to her bedchamber, only to find her curled up under the covers, fast asleep.

So she wouldn't be needing tea any time

soon.

He sat down on the chair beneath the window and stared at her. He'd never seen her this close before, and she was more beautiful than he remembered. Her voice was more melodious, too. He'd only heard her speak once before, with her brother, when…

When William Steel said she'd killed him.

Carline had killed him.

Most men he knew would wrap their hands around her neck and choke the life out of her for that. Naught but self defence, really, if she'd tried to kill him.

But he couldn't bring himself to do it. Even if she had killed him, which made him…what? Not an angel. A demon, maybe, for he did not recall having wings and horns before he'd died.

A cunning man would ravish her as she slept, so she'd have no choice but to marry him, or be ruined. Then again, he had no need to even touch her — just his presence, alone with her in her bedchamber, would mean her ruin, should anyone know of it.

But he couldn't bring himself to ravish her, either. Some demon he was – weren't demons supposed to steal maidens' virtue, every chance they got? Or at least torment them?

This was not going at all like he'd imagined. He'd meant to steal her, and then when they were well away from her brother, he'd explain to her how much he loved her and how he meant to marry her. She'd come to love him as he loved her, and willingly invite him into her bed where he'd…well, ravish her.

Maybe that's what she'd been about to do, when she began undressing, only he'd left to make tea and…

God, he was a fool. Now it was too late to ask her, because she was asleep.

He'd just have to sit there and wait for her to wake, then. Nodding to himself, Stan resolved to do just that.

TWENTY

"Please wake up. It's almost dawn and I must speak with you."

That Voice. She'd slept with him, hadn't she?

A pity she didn't remember any of it. A guy with a voice that hot should be at least passable in bed. Not forgettable.

Let's see…she'd gone to the cemetery with the girls, and then the security guard had come, and she'd twisted her ankle. She'd distracted the security guard while the other girls got away and then…she remembered wings and horns on a rooftop.

But no sex at all.

She wasn't even naked. She'd put on her My Little Pony pyjamas that no man was ever supposed to see. Yet here she was wearing them, and he was still here.

Which meant he was not only forgettable in bed, but he was probably about as attractive as the back end of a bunyip. A one night stand that would never be repeated.

Better get this over with, then.

She forced her eyes open.

Oh wow. More like the front end of a bunyip, if bunyips had horns and wings and…was that a six…no, definitely an eight pack.

"Please. I only have a few minutes before the sun comes up."

"What happens when the sun comes up?" she asked.

"I turn to stone in sunlight, and don't turn back until after sunset," he replied. "Which is why…"

Alethea nodded slowly. She might not remember much of last night, but she did know her way around her parents' apartment. "Okay, so if we block out the sunlight, that'll buy us some time, right?"

He nodded.

"Then we need to close the shutters." She slid over to the side of the bed and set her feet on the ground. Only to find that one ankle had swollen up twice the size of the other one – no way was she putting any weight on that. "Move the curtain on that side. There's a switch next to the window."

He followed where she was pointing, and found the switch. "This?"

"Yes. Flick that and the shutter should come down."

With a protesting whine, the shutter slid into place, shrouding the room in darkness.

"There's a switch like that and a shutter on

every window. If you close all the shutters, we solve the sunlight problem, yes?"

Again, he nodded.

"If we've only got a few minutes until dawn and my ankle's not going to get me anywhere fast, do you think you can close all the shutters in time?"

Quick as a shadow, he was gone.

By the time he returned, she'd turned on the bedside lamp and hopped to the bathroom and back.

"You should not be walking if you're injured. You should have waited for me to carry you," he said, frowning.

Yeah, he had a point. Especially as her ankle was throbbing now. She should have grabbed some pain pills while she was in the bathroom, like she had last night. Oh, maybe that's why she didn't remember anything – the pills had knocked her out. Which made it even weirder that he was still here.

"Look, I need to know one thing first, before anything else. Did we sleep together last night?" she asked.

He started to shake his head.

"We didn't have sex?" she persisted. Well, that would explain why she didn't remember it. Getting up close and personal with a body like that was something she figured she'd definitely remember.

"Of course not," he said, looking affronted.

Alethia allowed herself to relax, just a little. "So what are you doing in my bedroom then?"

"I am your demon protector. You summoned me, and I told you this last night."

Yeah, she remembered that. She'd kind of hoped it was a dream, though.

"So the horns and the wings are all real, then?"

They looked real. All of him looked pretty damn real, even if he did belong on a book cover more than her parents' bedroom.

"Of course I am real, woman! Would I be standing here, in your bedchamber, waiting to discuss an important matter with you, if I was not real?" he growled.

Oh hell. When he growled in That Voice…now she understood how it was possible for underwear to melt. Or dissolve. Or spontaneously combust…

She shook her head to clear it. Of course. He'd woken her up because he needed to speak to her, hadn't he? She'd had her questions answered, but he was still waiting. Demons weren't known for their patience.

"Okay, so how about you take a seat, and we can talk about whatever it was that was so urgent, you needed to wake me up for it," Alethea said.

"I prefer to stand."

Actually, he seemed to prefer to pace the length of the room, his tail swishing behind him, like some sort of caged beast, or maybe just the Bell House cat, but Alethia just nodded.

Finally, he planted himself directly in front of her, his piercing stare capturing her gaze. "Why did you kill me, Carline?"

TWENTY-ONE

She just stared at him, like she didn't understand a word he'd just said. "What?" she said finally.

He was fast losing patience with her. Surely she didn't think he was a fool. "Don't mess with me, Carline. The last thing I remember before I died is your brother saying, very distinctly, that you'd killed me. What I want to know is why."

She nodded slowly, looking thoughtful. After a long moment, she said slowly, "All right. Is there anything else you remember, like what year this happened?"

Ah, so perhaps some time had passed since that fateful night, and her memory of it was not as clear as his. He must remedy matters, then. "It was the winter of 1834, shortly after the natives raided your brother's mill on the southern side of the river from Perth town. You must remember it." He wished he could remember more, but his memories past that last night were terribly hazy.

More nodding. "All right. Now, do you have a name, Mr Demon Protector, or what should I call you?"

Stan blew out a breath. God, she must think him a rude brute, and she'd be right. He hadn't even bothered to introduce himself.

He bowed low. "Please forgive me. I am Stanley Steel. Stan, if you wish."

"Stan – if I may call you Stan – this might come as a bit of a shock to you, but some time has passed since your death in 1834."

It was his turn to nod. Of course. He'd already come to that conclusion. It also explained why he could not use her kitchen.

"It's now the year 2020."

The…wait, what did she say?

"My name is Alethia Bell. I don't have a brother, and I've never killed anyone, least of all you. Also, I don't remember any attack on the Old Mill at South Perth, but as 1834 was a bit before my time, I hope you understand why I wasn't there."

Oh God. This was…he'd almost… "You're not Carline?" he blurted out.

A faint smile lifted her lips. "No, I'm not Carline, who doesn't sound like a very nice person if she killed you. I really am Alethia Bell. Well, Alethia Caroline Bell, if you want to be precise, but not Carline Bell."

"Carline Steel. Her name was Carline Steel," he said. Then he shook his head. "But you look just like her." The white gold hair, the well-rounded figure…

"Steel. A relative, then?" Alethia enquired.

"Second cousin. We were to be married," Stan said. Well, if his plan had succeeded. If Carline hadn't killed him…

"Was she…look, Stan, you seem like a nice enough guy and all, but if she killed you, I have to ask…was she happy about your engagement?" She looked almost afraid of what his answer might be.

Stan closed his eyes. "She didn't even know."

Alethia blew out a breath. "Well, so much for that as her motive. If she were still alive, we could ask her, but if she was around in 1834, she probably isn't around now. Look, I want to help you, especially after you helped me get home last night, but it's pretty early to be solving a nearly two hundred year old murder mystery. Especially if it's your murder, which I imagine is about as personal as these things get. So, I propose we both take a minute to think about that for a bit, and then we can regroup after I've had a shower. Maybe over coffee and breakfast?"

"A shower?" What did rain have to do with anything? And how could she possess rain?

"Ah. Yeah, not something they had here in 1834, I imagine. Um, I'm going to go into that room over there and wash. Naked."

Stan swallowed. A hundred times while she'd slept, he'd imagined her naked. He'd thought she was Carline, who he'd been dreaming about for years, but still…

"Do you…do you need my assistance with that?" he choked out. He couldn't even decide what he wanted her response to be.

She stared at him for a long moment, as through she was reading his mind. Perhaps she was. Finally, she said, "You know, I can't tell if that's supposed to be a come-on, or if you genuinely want to help."

Well, that made two of them.

She held up both hands. "I can probably hop in there by myself, and sit on the little plastic stool I've been using to shave my legs, and hop back here okay. But if you'd be willing to carry me to the kitchen, that I wouldn't refuse."

"Then I will do as you wish, Miss Bell."

"Alethia. I wish for you to call me Alethia."

He grinned. "Alethia, then."

She might not be Carline, but she was every bit as beautiful as Carline had been. Plus, she was alive and she already seemed to like him. After all, she hadn't even tried to kill him yet. And she had no brother to threaten his life for daring to look at her.

TWENTY-TWO

Alethia waited until the hot shower spray drowned out any noise she might make, before she sank onto the shower tiles and burst out laughing. It was partly hysterical laughter, but she had to admit it was funny.

Last night, she'd gotten drunk with the girls and summoned a hot demon, who she definitely had not had sex with, who was not only still here the next morning, but he wanted her help solving a murder mystery. Funnier still, for a moment there, after he'd offered to help her in the shower, she could have sworn there was a wicked glint in his eye that said if she wanted the sex they hadn't had last night, at a word from her, he'd absolutely come and give her the hottest shower she'd ever had.

And she'd almost agreed to have steamy sex with a demon. Until she'd gathered up her lost wits and forced herself to say she was showering alone.

Of course, he was probably still sitting there in the bedroom, waiting for her. If she was to ask him for help…

Her wild imagination offered up a tantalising image of him backing her up against the bathroom wall, plunging deep inside her until she screamed his name in ecstasy.

Stanley Steel. Not the sort of name she'd expected for a demon, but then he'd been human once, hadn't he? In 1834. Right at the start of the Swan River Colony.

She took her time in the shower, even

shaving her legs, which she usually didn't bother to do in winter, but if she wrapped her legs around his waist, she wanted them smooth as silk.

Of course, she'd probably imagined that glint, she decided, as she dried off and dressed. She'd read far too many paranormal and alien romances to believe that any hot-blooded creature who wasn't a normal human male would absolutely be looking for love and filled with lust for whatever lady he first saw. But that didn't stop her from wanting it to be true.

He was waiting for her when she opened the bathroom door, appreciative eyes taking her in as if a stretchy sweater and a pair of leggings were the sexiest thing he'd seen all year. Well, if he'd been stuck in hell, maybe it was.

He didn't look so bad himself – in nothing but a pair of jeans that hung low on his hips, so his tail could swing free. "Shall I carry you to the kitchen?" He held out his arms.

"Yes, please."

His arms around her felt just as good as they had last night. Wait, hadn't they landed on a rooftop on the way?

"Did you fly me home last night?" she asked.

He set her down on one of the dining chairs. "Of course. Much faster than walking."

"Or hopping." Which she did, to reach the kitchen bench and the coffee machine. Her parents usually ordered a whole selection of pods, but she stuck to two – the mocha, and the caramel ones. This morning, she picked a mocha one.

While the machine did its magic, she turned to face Stanley. "So, what would you like for breakfast? My parents had a standing order for a weekly farm produce box, only they forget to cancel it, and the first one was so good, I just kept going. The delivery came yesterday, so on top of the usual cereal, milk and toast, I have apples, blueberry muffins, a sourdough with olives, some jam I haven't really looked at yet, and a massive jar of honey. Oh, and some sort of creamy, spreadable cheese that I wanted to try on some toasted sourdough."

Stan just shook his head in wonder. "So many things I've never even heard of, let alone tasted. The colony truly has flourished, just like I said it would. If only I could enjoy its bounty, as I'm sure you do, but I have no need for any of it."

Alethea's mouth dropped open. "What, demons don't eat? I mean, I've never met a demon before, but this is the first time I've heard they don't need to eat. Or that they turn to stone in sunlight. I thought that was trolls, not demons. What else about demons do I need to know?"

Stan shrugged. "I don't need to eat or drink, so you don't need to cook on my account, though that coffee does smell quite delicious. I can fly, of course, but you already knew that. I don't know what to tell you — I don't know any other demons."

"You mean you didn't see any demons in hell? What's it like there, then, if there aren't any demons?" Alethea asked.

Another shrug. "I don't remember. All I remember is the night I died…and then you summoning me."

"But you remember the early days of the colony," she said eagerly. So many things she wanted to ask him, she wasn't sure what to ask first.

Stan shook his head. "I remember one night, and even that's hazy. I could not even remember how to make you a cup of tea last night."

"Good thing I don't drink tea, then. Callie's the tea drinker. I prefer coffee, but I like it sweet." She topped her cup up with milk, then held it up in a toast. "What should we drink to? I mean, normally it's to good health, but you're a demon and I've twisted my ankle, so that seems pretty pointless right now."

Stan frowned. "You should not be standing on your injured foot. Do you have what you need for breakfast?"

Alethia grabbed a blueberry muffin in her

free hand. "Now I do."

He scooped her up, then carried her back to the dining table, so smoothly she didn't even spill her coffee.

"I didn't know nursing duties were part of being a demon protector. Or is this just you, going above and beyond? Because I haven't even known you a day and I can tell you, you are definitely the best protector, demon or otherwise, that I've ever had." She raised her coffee mug to him before she drank.

A sad smile appeared on his face. "If only Carline had agreed with you."

"Oh, Stan." She reached out and squeezed his hand. "I'm sorry things didn't work out for you and Carline. But I'll tell you what. While you're here protecting me, I'll help you find out what happened that night, if I can, and maybe even work out why she killed you. It's the least I can do."

"But how can you possibly find out something that happened almost two hundred years ago, when everyone who was there is dead?" He didn't make an exception for himself, either.

Alethea grinned. "Well, it just so happens that you are the demon protector to an archaeologist who specialises in early Swan River colonial history. Why, only yesterday I was digging up the bodies of some of our earliest Scottish settlers." Oh hell, had she dug up his body? She hoped not. "I have contacts everywhere historical documents are stored, and if it's on the internet, I can and will find it. And seeing as there's no way I'll be able to go to work for a few days until my ankle heals, you will have exclusive use of my services for the foreseeable future."

He stared down at her hand atop his, where it still sat. "We have a deal," he said slowly. "I will protect you, and you will help me."

Alethea almost choked on her coffee. She'd just made a deal with a demon.

TWENTY-THREE

She wasn't Carline. If some benevolent angel hadn't been watching over him last night, he might have ravished the wrong woman.

Not that he would have minded, for she was every bit as beautiful as Carline, and she didn't seem to mind that he was a demon. Which made her an even greater temptation. One he needed to avoid.

Because if he truly was back on earth to be

Alethia's protector, then someone had given him a second chance. A chance to redeem himself, so that maybe he wouldn't be sent back to hell, and he'd be allowed to go elsewhere instead. To where he might be reunited with Carline.

Which, of course, meant he had to be on his best behaviour in every way. To be the best, most dedicated protector Alethia could possibly have. The sort of protector he'd wanted to be for Carline, if she'd let him.

"Could you pass me my laptop, please? It's in that bag." Alethea pointed.

Stan could see the bag, but he had no idea what a laptop might be, so he scooped up the bag and set it on the table before her.

"That works." She reached into her bag and pulled out what Stan took to be some sort of folio. Sure enough, when she opened it, the top part appeared to be a highly polished slate, while the part that still rested on the table resembled a printing press with all the letters laid out on it. Then Alethia swiped her fingers across the slate and…

"How did you do that?" Stan asked, peering at the picture that had appeared on the slate.

"That? Oh, that's one of the mountain ranges up north, near one of the mine sites. One of the guys at work is a drone pilot and in between surveying the site from the air, he took a bunch of aerial shots, too. This one's my favourite because the colour of the rocks contrasts so strongly with the ocean in the background. Of course, the water's only there on the really high tides, because a few hours later, it looked like this." She tapped the slate and the picture changed, with white sand where the teal waters had been.

"But how do you make such pictures appear? It's like looking through a window at this place from a great height. Like looking through the eyes of a bird. Is this witchcraft?"

Alethia laughed. "No witchcraft, just modern technology. Um, you're looking at a picture of the scene, captured by a flying device, which then sends the information through to a laptop like mine. So many things I imagine you just didn't have in 1834, and I'm probably the worst person ever to try to explain how they work to you. I mean, I'm an archaeologist. My job is to dig up and explain objects from the past to present-day people. I never expected I'd have to explain present-day objects to someone from the past. What I was hoping to do is see if there are any online records of your Carline. Carline Steel, right?"

Stan nodded.

The picture on the slate vanished, to be replaced by a lot of words. Alethia tapped her fingers on the letters beneath the slate, and Carline's name appeared on the slate. A tiny arrow moved across the screen to touch the word SEARCH before everything vanished, only to be replaced by a new selection of words.

Alethia peered at the slate, muttering to herself as she read.

"Right, it says here she arrived with her brother William Steel in 1829, then married

Sean Bell in 1834. She died in…1887. Sorry, Stan."

Carline had died an old woman, after a long and likely happy life, with someone else, while he'd…he'd…

Alethia leaned over and threw her arms around him, hugging him tightly. "I'm so sorry, Stan."

He had to force himself to unclench his fists before he could hug her back. If he closed his eyes, or merely fixed them on the silvery-blonde braid that hung down her back, he could almost believe she was Carline, and the soft breasts crushed against his chest were…

No. This was Alethia, not Carline, and he was her protector, not her ravisher. He had to keep his desires in check, or he would never achieve redemption, and never see Carline again.

He pulled back, out of her embrace. It was better this way.

TWENTY-FOUR

Yep, she'd done it again. Forgotten not everyone was a hugger. Especially a huge horned, winged demon who'd grown up during the Regency. If she remembered her Jane Austen right, touching a man with your bare hand or just being alone with him was enough to ruin a woman.

Then again, he hadn't exactly been wearing gloves – or anything at all – when he carried her home last night. And he'd spent the whole night naked in her bedroom. Her eyes darted to his groin, the one place she'd been trying to avoid looking at…

"Where did you get those?" she asked. He definitely hadn't been wearing those low-slung jeans last night.

He glanced down. "They were in a small room adjacent to your bedchamber, with a lot of other men's clothing. I had intended to don a shirt, too, but all the ones I found were too small."

That explained why the jeans fit so snugly, then. They had to be her dad's, and no way would any of Dad's shirts fit Stan's broad shoulders. And his muscles would probably rip right through the sleeves.

"I hope the owner of these does not object to me borrowing them while I protect you," Stan said, frowning.

"I doubt Dad will ever fit into his old jeans again, especially not now he's probably augmenting that beer belly with a wine and cheese belly." She bet they were having an awesome time.

"Where is your father now? If he returns, then surely I must hide, for he will not approve of a demon's presence anywhere near his daughter, even if I am your protector," Stan said.

Alethia laughed. Her dad didn't believe in demons, so he'd probably try to interrogate Stan, either out of curiosity or the desire to catch him in a lie. "My parents are in France, touring snail farms and shopping at farmers markets and all the things you do when you don't have to work and you're staying in the French countryside."

"And they would leave you here alone?" Stan looked shocked.

"I'm a grown woman, Stan, with a job and a life of my own. When I don't have a twisted ankle, I usually get along by myself just fine."

"But what would they say if they knew you were consorting with demons?"

"Dad would probably ask you a whole

bunch of questions, and Mum…well, she'd probably say you're an improvement over the last guy I tried to date. Better looking. More polite. And not a crazy stalker who wants me to have his babies, which is always a plus. He's the reason Callie suggested we try to summon you, actually. To protect me from him."

Stan's expression turned thunderous. "There is a man stalking you? One who means to ravish you?"

It was Alethia's turn to frown. "I don't know about the ravishing part. Come to think of it, I thought you said we didn't do any consorting last night. Now you're telling me we did do something?" But surely she'd remember. Or at least ache a bit afterwards, because Stan definitely wasn't small.

He drew himself up. "I'm sure I don't know what you mean."

"Fuck." She rubbed her forehead with her fingers, hoping to stave off the threatening headache. Dealing with two hundred year old demons was hard. Sex education for a Regency man was torture. "Okay, let me be completely clear, then. Consorting, ravishing, sleeping, whatever euphemism you use…it all amounts to sex, right? Penises and vaginas and a whole lot of thrusting. Maybe involving some other body parts, too, to keep it interesting. But in its most basic form, sexual intercourse between a man and a woman is when your dick goes into her vagina. Or…other places." She fought not to blush at the image that popped into her head, of her going down on him and then him reciprocating. Her cheeks might not be growing uncomfortably hot, but other places sure were. Wet, too. Alethia closed her eyes. "Did we, or did we not, have sex last night?"

"We most certainly did not."

Oh, now she'd offended him. Yeah, two hundred years ago, well-born ladies didn't talk about private parts, or what you did with them.

"And if this man stalking you so much as thinks he could do such a thing with you, I will crush him," Stan said. "I am your protector, and this is my purpose. No man will ruin you while I am with you."

Not even him. Alethia sighed. "Thanks, Stan."

TWENTY-FIVE

Alethia's attention was on her laptop, as she called the strange device with the words and pictures, so she didn't notice when he rose and began pacing her tenement. Most likely her parents' tenement, and not hers at all, he decided as he surveyed his surroundings, for the majority of it was dusty, as if it had not been used for some months. The exceptions were the bedchamber, the room she'd called the bathroom, and the large chamber with a kitchen at one end where she currently sat.

There was a second slate, much larger than the one she was presently staring at, hanging on the wall before a large sofa. "Does this slate show pictures, too?" he asked.

Alethia glanced up. "Well, yes, because that's a television. I could put something on for you to watch if you like, but most programs would leave you with more questions than answers. I think there's a slideshow of pictures from around the world that pops up if you pause it for too long." She rose, picked up a slim black box, about an inch wide and as long as her hand, and pointed it at the slate. A succession of unfamiliar words and pictures flashed across the screen, until a snow-capped mountain appeared. "There you go." Her gaze returned to the laptop.

Stan wasn't sure whether to ignore the slate and keep walking, or whether he was supposed to look at the pictures. The mountain looked so real, so clear, it was almost impossible to believe he wasn't looking out a window at the scene. Then the view changed, into a landscape just as mesmerising as the first.

Countless pictures later, Stan blinked, suddenly aware of Alethea calling his name. "Forgive me, I was distracted by the pictures. What is it you need?"

"Don't feel bad. Everyone gets distracted by the TV. Come over here and see what I've managed to find so far."

Stan moved to stand behind her, peering at her small slate over her shoulder, where a whitewashed windmill appeared.

"Do you recognise this?" she asked.

Stan shook his head. "Carline's brother's mill was made of wood, not stone, and it was not painted. There were no buildings beneath it, either – just a tent, where the two of them lived."

"Yeah, it says this mill – which we call the Old Mill, funnily enough, was the second one built on the site in 1835, after the first one burned down. But that's the only reference I can find to the burning. Do you think maybe you died in the fire? That Carline didn't kill you at all, and it was an accident?"

There was no fire. Even the cookfire had been extinguished. "There was no fire that night."

"The other funny thing is that there's no record of Carline Steel's arrival. Her brother William Steel came on the *HMS Sulphur*, and it says he had a wife, but not her name."

"There were only two beds in that tent. His, and hers. There was no wife. Either she died in the early days of the colony, or Carline was pretending to be his wife for some reason." Stan wet his lips. "I'd heard stories about her being a witch, but I never believed them. If someone else did, though, and came after her for it…perhaps she fled to the colony to hide from the false accusations, and said she was her brother's wife to hide her identity." Which made little sense, for there was very little difference between Miss or Mrs Steel. "I do not know."

"Then there's this Sean Bell. There are several mentions of a Sean Bell throughout the years, though they can't possibly be the same man. He apparently arrived on the *Hooghly* in 1830, but his name doesn't appear on the passenger list. Yours does, though. Do you remember a man by that name?"

Stan shook his head. "I remember nothing of ships, or anyone aboard them."

"There is a Mr Bell who arrived on the *Calista* in 1829, six months earlier, and that could have been him. He was granted land in 1834, the same year he married Miss Steel, where they built Bell Cottage. Almost eighty years later, after a bushfire had burned Bell Cottage, another Sean Bell built Bell House, which still stands. It can't be the same man, because he'd have been more than a hundred when Bell House was built. I can't find any death or burial record for either of them, though. I mean, no record for the first guy I understand because cemetery records were pretty patchy in the beginning. But the Sean who built Bell House would be more than a hundred years old now, if he were still alive, so there should be some modern day record of something, but there's nothing. Not even a death date or year for either of them." She swallowed. "There isn't a death date or burial for you, either. I know you said you died in 1834, but…there's no record of any burial. Because we've been working at the East Perth Cemeteries site, I have the complete database of everyone buried there, since the colony began, and your name isn't there."

Stan spread his hands wide. "I don't know what to say. I'm sorry, but I don't remember where my body was buried. I was dead at that point."

She began to laugh. "Oh God, of course you were. I just figured because you appeared at East Perth Cemeteries, you must have been buried there. Or maybe you were one of the undocumented burials. With no record and no headstone, your body could have been buried anywhere, and we'd never find it."

"Why would I want to? That body is dead. This one is as strong as mine ever was, maybe even stronger. Good enough to be your protector, which is all I need it for," Stan said.

She stared at him for a long moment. "You really don't want to dig up the past, do you? I've found an anomaly, a gap in history, a bunch of missing bodies and a mystery I'm dying to solve, but you, even though you're central to the mystery, and your body is one of the ones I'm searching for, you don't care. The only part of any of it that matters to you is why Carline killed you. You're like my exact opposite, in every possible way."

Definitely not Carline. He couldn't believe he'd once mistaken Alethia for her. "It doesn't matter. What matters is the present. Why don't you tell me about this man stalking you. The more I know, the better I can protect you."

TWENTY-SIX

"So I ran all the way home," Alethia finished. "Look, I probably wouldn't have reacted quite so strongly on any other day, but I was already freaked out, so I freaked out a bit more. When I got home, I called the girls, who said they'd come over, and…well…now you're here."

Stan's expression didn't look like it could get any darker. "I will find this man, and I will ensure you never set eyes upon him again."

"That sounds ominous. How exactly do you plan to do that?"

"Through any means necessary."

That sounded worse. "Stan, I'm going to need specifics here. Times have changed, and things that might have been acceptable when you were alive are…different now. So tell me exactly what you have planned, and I'll tell you whether it's a good idea or not."

"Such things are not fit for a lady's ears," Stan said stiffly.

"Well, there's no ladies here, buster. I dig up dead bodies for a living. I've seen shit you can't even imagine, and not just in movies, either." She rose to her feet, then winced as her ankle protested. "Now, are you my protector or aren't you?"

Stan bowed his head. "As I keep telling you, I am your demon protector. Bound to serve you."

"Well, can you see my ankle all swelled up? The person I'm in greatest danger from right now is me. I keep forgetting I'm injured and trying to walk on it."

Stan scooped her up in his arms and marched down the passage. "Then I shall carry you to bed, and see that you stay there."

"Uh huh, and who's going to cook while I'm stuck in bed? Carry me over to the couch. It's Saturday morning. Pretty sure I'm allowed to spend the day binge watching stuff, and maybe bring you up to speed on how much the world has changed since you were last part of it. Put me down there and pass me the remote."

Stan set her down, then stood in front of her, looking at a loss.

"What are you doing?" she asked. Now there was a wall of muscle with wings between her and the TV.

"Protecting you from yourself."

She had to laugh at that. "You can do that and watch TV, you know. Sit here, next to me." She patted the couch beside her.

"That would not be seemly."

Alethia sighed. "Look, Stan, I know things

were different in your time. Just being alone with me last night was enough to ruin me, by the standards of your time, right?"

He shifted on his feet and wouldn't meet her eyes. "Well, yes, but no one knows I was here, so your reputation is safe. If I were to sit beside you, an unmarried woman, it would not be seemly."

"Okay, then…so if you won't sit on the couch, maybe the floor, then? So we can both see the screen."

Stan's gaze followed her pointing finger. "But the pictures are no longer on the slate."

Alethia waved the remote control. "I can bring them back. Just remember, if you decide maybe the couch is okay after all, there's plenty of space for you."

"I will not change my mind."

"Suit yourself."

She flipped through the options. She'd been all ready to watch *Supernatural* with the girls last night, but it seemed insensitive to watch the Winchesters kill demons when there was an actual demon in the room who'd been a perfect gentleman since he'd first appeared. Maybe something supernatural without the capital S. She clicked through to suggestions, and then had to choke back a laugh. A gentleman from the past who finds himself suddenly in the present, thanks to some supernatural assistance…yes, *Sleepy Hollow* should work just fine. It'd been ages since she'd watched it, and she did remember liking it when she had.

Less than a minute in, Stan folded his arms across his chest. "How is this possible? Seeing a battle from the past as though we were only looking out a window upon it."

Yep, the pause button was going to get a workout today.

"It's not real. It's…actors in costumes, with pretend weapons. Like in a play. Only the camera — the same device that took the picture of the mountains you saw on my laptop — filmed it, so we could watch it again whenever we want."

"But it looks real."

"The actors and the film crew did a really good job, then."

She waited to see if he had any more questions, before she allowed the show to play again.

Huh. She'd forgotten the hero'd had to dig his way out of his own grave. Had Stan had to do that? Was that why he wasn't worried about where his body was buried, because there was no body left to find? All those empty graves in the cemetery…how many were empty because they'd been summoned as demons? Alethia shivered. This sort of thing was what you expected in America, or Eastern Europe, or in movies, but not here in Western Australia.

"Those are modern horseless carriages, are they not?"

Alethia had to force her thoughts back to what was on the TV. She nodded. "Yes. A truck and a car, respectively, on a modern highway, like the ones we flew over when you brought me home."

"But this is more like a gothic novel, yes? It is not real?"

"Like a novel, or a play, yeah."

"So the man with no head is…?"

Alethia grinned. "An American legend, from a story that's about as old as you, I believe."

"I heard stories of a horseman who carried his head about in his saddlebag when I was a boy, back in Scotland. In some tales, he was a man, killed in one of the clan battles for the isles. In others, he was not a man at all, but a fae creature who collects the dead. There is also Sir Gawain and the Green Knight, a tale that is older than the discovery of the Americas. My mother was fond of this particular tale, and I read it aloud many times."

Alethia blinked. For a man who claimed he could only remember his dying moments, that was a whole bunch of new memories…with not a single mention of Carline. Evidently she'd made a good choice of TV show for Stan, at least.

"There's so many lights in your time. On

the carriages, all over the houses, in the streets! The only time I've seen so many lights was when we went to Glasgow, and they were gaslights, my da said, burning gas that came from coal."

"Yeah, gaslights were a thing for a while, but now most lighting is electric. Like…lightning, but through wires. I learned how it worked back in high school science class, but that was a while ago, so I'm not sure I'd be able to explain it to you any better than that."

Stan grinned up at her. "I could not explain how gaslights work, either. It was not something a Scottish farm boy needed to know."

Ah, so that's how a demon wound up with a Scottish accent. Actually, he didn't look so demonic right now. It took her a moment to realise why.

"Your wings are gone!"

Stan shrugged, his eyes on the TV screen. "I put them away. It's easier to sit down and lean against your chair without them. It's the same with the tail."

He'd vanished his horns, too, and without all the extra bits, he looked almost human. Well, still hot as hell in his shirtless state, but the kind of hot that made her wish he would join her on the couch, and then one thing would lead to another, and…

Stop perving on your demon protector, she scolded herself. If he was even the slightest bit interested, he'd be on the couch already.

TWENTY-SEVEN

After several hours of watching the slate Alethia called a television, she stretched and said, "Lunchtime, I think. Are you sure I can't get you anything?"

"No, but I should carry you to the kitchen." He knew what they'd watched wasn't real, but there was one part of it he'd wished was real, for he wouldn't feel so useless if it were. She'd probably think he was silly, having to ask for her help, but… "Would you show me how to use the things in your kitchen? If I only knew how your coffee machine worked, or perhaps even your stove, I might be able to do some of the work, to keep you off that ankle."

"You mean like if I stuck sticky notes to everything with instructions on how to use it? I was actually thinking about that when I saw it, only I'm not sure if my parents have any sticky notes in the house. Maybe in Dad's office…"

"I'll carry you there first." If she was willing, he'd do everything to make it easier for her. He needed to be the best protector possible, which meant adjusting to the numerous strange devices in this time.

In a room that was more of a library than an office, at least in Stan's opinion, Alethia found a small notepad that she declared was good enough, along with something she called a pen that didn't look like any writing implement Stan had ever seen before. Yet when he set her on one of the chairs at the dining table, she began writing with it immediately, with no inkwell in sight.

Yet another magical modern invention he had no hope of understanding.

Each time she tore off a page, she'd hand it to him to stick in its proper place. On the coffee maker. On the stove. On the fridge, whatever that was. The freezer. The tap for water. The kettle.

"I think the dishwasher might be a bit too complicated to explain on one sticky note. Maybe I'll just leave that until we fill it up or run out of plates and actually use it."

Stan could barely believe what he was hearing. "There is a device that washes dishes for you?"

"Yes, and one that washes clothes, too. Even one that dries them, which has been a godsend here, where there's no space on the balcony for a clothesline. Not like where I used to live, where you could turn the whole wraparound veranda into your washing line, rain, hail or shine."

"If only there was a device that could cook

all your meals for you, too, then women would never have to do any work in the kitchen ever again!" Stan exclaimed.

Alethia looked uncomfortable. "Well, Mum has something like that. A something mix, I think it's called. It's supposed to prepare and cook and stir your food, if you just put the right ingredients in. That's when Mum uses it, anyway. I'm not much of a cook, and the one time I tried it, it just kept beeping at me and telling me I'd made an error. I finally decided my only mistake was in thinking I could cook with it in the first place, so I ordered pizza. Which is probably what I'll do tonight, too, unless you happen to have some amazing cooking skills you haven't yet told me about?" Now she looked hopeful.

He hated to disappoint her. "I can make fish stew in a pot over the fire, mostly without burning it. I can catch and gut the fish, too."

She laughed. "That officially makes you a better cook than me."

"You haven't tasted it." He couldn't

remember the taste of it, either. He only knew that he'd choked it down because it was that or nothing, and he'd been so determined to live, to succeed, that he'd have done almost anything to ensure he did. And it still hadn't been enough. Carline had killed him, and married another man. What else could he have done that he hadn't already?

"What do you mean?" Alethia asked, wrinkling her nose in confusion.

Too late, Stan realised he'd spoken the words aloud. He opened his mouth to tell her it was nothing, and to forget what he'd said, but something told him Alethia's curiosity would not be so easily deflected.

Sure enough…

"You asked what else you could have done that you hadn't already. I can't answer you unless you tell me what you did, and why you did it. I still might not be any help, especially if it's to do with cooking, but at least I can try!" She folded her arms across her chest, her mulish expression telling him he would not be able to disobey this order. "Now, explain."

Stan swallowed. Though Alethia looked nothing like his mother, he was reminded of that time he'd torn his trousers when she could ill afford to replace them. Size and strength meant nothing when a woman could inspire terror just with the tone of her voice.

"I did everything I could to make myself a worthy husband for Carline, and it was not enough," he said quietly. "Even cook and eat that foul fish stew for months while we were camping in Clarence Town. There was nothing I would not do, and yet everything I did was not enough to save her being married off to someone else. I was wondering what else I could have done to make her my wife."

Alethia bit her lip and held out her hands to him. For a moment, he hesitated, before he took her small hands in his. Strong hands, for all their softness and diminutive size. Then she looked up at him and he was caught in her gaze, a moth to her inexplicable inner flame.

"I don't know why some relationships fail,

while others last for life. Why one person thinks another is their soul mate, when the other person has no feelings for the first at all. I can't speak for Carline, because I never met her. But I do know that sometimes two people aren't destined to be together, no matter how much one of them wishes it to be so. The guy stalking me is convinced we're soul mates, and I know we're not. There's nothing he can do to convince me. Maybe it's the same with you and Carline. There was no spark…"

"But I never even got to find out! I never even got to speak to her!" Stan said. "If I'd even had a chance to woo her, for even a minute…"

"How could you possibly fall in love with someone you've never even spoken to?" Alethia asked.

"I just knew! From the moment I saw her…" Stan swallowed. That was why his heart leaped every time he looked at Alethia, because she looked so much like her. Even if she was…softer.

Alethia sighed. "Look, if this were a romance novel, I'd believe you, because love at first sight and instalove are definitely a thing in those, but…even if those do exist in real life, it kind of has to be a two-way thing for it to actually work. I'll tell you what. I'll take another look into some of my more obscure sources after lunch, and see if there's anything I missed. Well, aside from the obvious, of course."

Stan hadn't understood half of what she'd said. "What's obvious?" he asked.

"She married Sean Bell, and they built Bell Cottage, which was later replaced by Bell House. Your Carline and her husband were my many-times great-grandparents. It's probably why I remind you of her."

Stan reared back. Carline's granddaughter? That made Alethia some sort of cousin. More distant than Carline, but still…family. Of course he had to protect her.

"No matter what you find, I will protect you," he promised, knowing Carline would approve.

TWENTY-EIGHT

Alethia woke up with her head resting on something harder than her usual pillow, though the warm blanket around her shoulders was delightfully soft. She blinked, then blinked some more before her mind managed to wrap around the reality: some time during the afternoon, Stan had joined her on the couch, and she was now using his chest for a pillow, while he'd draped his wings, which had magically reappeared, around her in a sort of leathery cocoon that made her envy caterpillars in a whole new way.

The TV had turned itself off at some point. She probably should have told Stan how the remote control worked. Then again, she hadn't exactly expected to fall asleep on him and pin him to the couch for hours of boredom with nothing to watch.

"What time is it?" she mumbled.

"It is 6:35 in the evening, according to that clock." His voice rumbling in her ear sent shivers down her spine. If he'd added something about it being the perfect time for Netflix and chill, she'd straddle him in a heartbeat.

Down, girl, Alethia told herself. It had taken him hours to agree to share a couch with her. There was no way he was going to be amenable to hot sex any time soon.

Alethia sighed. "I should probably make dinner. Ooh, no, I was going to order pizza, wasn't I? Can you grab my laptop?"

Was she imagining it, or was he just as reluctant as she was to end their embrace? And that bulge in his jeans…no, she'd seen all of him last night. He was just naturally big, that was all. It didn't mean he was aching for sex as much as she was.

"Are you sure I can't get you anything?" she asked as she hovered the cursor over the SUBMIT ORDER button.

"Demons don't need food."

"Yeah, but…don't you still want it, though? I mean, the pizza place here is really good. Better than the one where I used to live. More pricey, too, but it's worth every cent. Which is why I usually eat a slice or two more than I need, because it's just so good."

Stan just shook his head, so she tapped the touchpad to place the order, then reached for the remote. "We have time for another episode before the pizza arrives, if you want?"

Stan stared at her. "Why do you wish to watch something that will only put you to sleep?"

Alethia couldn't remember the last time she'd fallen asleep in from of the TV, no matter what she'd been watching. It must have been the pain medication she took after lunch, which had already worn off, judging by the pain in her ankle when she moved. "It was the medicine I took that made me sleep. I'll stay awake, whatever we watch, I swear."

Sure enough, the episode's credits had just appeared when the intercom beeped to announce the pizza guy.

"Can you press the button to open the gate?" Alethia asked. When Stan just stared at her in bewilderment, she said, "Here, just lift me up and carry me over to the door, so I can show you."

The poor pizza guy was peering at the video screen, probably cursing her silently for taking so long, if his deep frown was anything to go by.

Feeling more like a fairytale princess than herself, Alethia pressed the intercom button. "Hi. Buzzing you up now." A moment later, the pizza guy disappeared from the front steps.

"More magic like your TV and your laptop?" Stan demanded.

Alethia laughed softly. "Technology more than magic, but I understand it might seem like magic to you. This time, the camera is at the front door, and the picture comes direct to this little screen when you press the button. You should probably put me down, so you can answer the door and have your hands free to take the pizza. Ah…the dining table, please."

By the time he'd helped her get plates and drinks out, a tentative knock sounded at the door.

"What do I do?" Stan asked. "I do not wish to compromise you, but you cannot walk without my help."

Alethia fought not to laugh. "Just open the door, take the boxes, thank the guy, and close the door again. It'll be fine."

"But do you not need to pay for your food? I have no coin from your time or mine."

Poor Stan. She really wanted to hug him,

but the two metres between them might have been the whole of Claisebrook Cove — too far for her to reach. "Don't worry, I've already paid."

"How?"

"Online credit card payment." At his look of confusion, she added, "Magic."

His frown only deepened. "I am not a fool. I know about credit. If Peel had not had good credit with his suppliers in Fremantle, he would have eaten a lot more fish stew with the rest of us who had no such privileges granted to us. Is it because you are Carline's granddaughter that shopkeepers give you credit?"

The knocking came again, louder this time. "Pizza for Alethia Bell!"

"Just get the pizza, please. I need food before I can properly explain the differences between Regency banking and how it works in the present day."

Stan threw open the door, startling the pizza guy. "Is this Miss Bell's meal?" he demanded.

"Uh, yeah." The pizza guy yanked the boxes out of the bag and thrust them at Stan's chest. "Have a good night, mate," he called over his shoulder as he bolted for the stairs.

Stan stared at the boxes in his hands, then at the fleeing pizza guy. "If you have poisoned or cursed this food, I will hunt you down and see that you regret it!" Stan called after him.

"Stan, please close the door and bring those here. It's not poisoned or cursed, but he won't deliver here again if you threaten him like that. Then you'll have to go pick it up from the shop instead, or I will, and even when my ankle's healed, I'm not going to want to walk all that way in the dark just to get a pizza that'll be cold by the time I get home, and I happen to like their pizza."

Grumbling under his breath, Stan obeyed, before planting himself on the dining chair across from her, arms folded across his chest and a scowl so deep his eyebrows met across his nose.

Alethia pulled out two slices and set them

on a plate, then waved it before him. "If you could taste it, you'd understand."

Stan sniffed. "It does smell…delicious."

"There's still enough for you, if you want it."

But he just shook his head.

"You're a stubborn demon, Stan, you know that? I bet you were a stubborn man, too." A sudden thought popped into her head, and before she could properly consider the ramifications, she said, "So, what did you actually do to earn a place in hell, anyway? It must have been pretty bad, to become a demon and all."

Stan muttered something under his breath. The only words Alethia could hear were "steal" and "Carline".

"What was that? You tried to steal from Carline? What did you steal from her? It must have been pretty valuable for her to want to kill you. Or to earn you a place in hell. I mean, trying to steal something isn't that bad. It's not like it's murder or…" Oh shit. What if…? She had to choose her words carefully now. "Stan, did you do something to Carline? Did you hurt her?"

Stan's face had gone as pale as the pizza box. "I didn't. I never…" He clenched both hands into fists and punched at the wall.

Alethia covered her head with her arms, expecting to be showered in plaster, but she didn't hear the impact. In fact, she didn't hear anything at all. When she raised her head, Stan was nowhere to be seen.

TWENTY-NINE

No. He'd never spoken to Carline, let alone touched her. He'd never have hurt her. Never. He'd intended to steal her to keep her safe.

Then what had he done to earn a place in hell?

Why couldn't he remember? Was it because he'd done something horrible, something that would justify the fear he'd seen in Alethia's eyes when she asked him what he'd done? He was her protector, just as he'd wanted to be Carline's. He would never have done something so terrible…

Yet here he was, a demon.

Stan was hardly aware of stepping through the wall until he stepped out of it again, into the next apartment. The Chinese woman who lived there had her back to him as she watched TV from her couch, the noise from the program drowning out any sound he made, but if she turned around…Stan slipped back inside the wall, his mind still whirling with thoughts he didn't want to have.

He couldn't have. He wouldn't. He'd never…

But the memories of that night didn't get any clearer.

Finally, he blew out a breath. Whatever had happened that night, he couldn't change it. Carline had killed him, and all he could do now was be the best protector possible, in the hope he might be able to claw his way out of hell. But to do that, he needed Alethia to trust him, not fear him.

Stan burst out of the wall. Alethia was still sitting at the dining table, where he'd left her, though the pizza on her plate was gone.

He dropped to his knees beside her, seizing her hand in both of his.

He thanked each and every deity in the universe that she didn't pull away, though her eyes widened in surprise. Surprise, not fear, he told himself, even if he didn't entirely believe it.

"Alethia, I swear to you, my sole purpose here is to protect you. Whatever I may have done in the past to earn my place in hell, it is nothing compared to what I will do to anyone who threatens you. I never touched Carline, nor did I do anything to hurt her. I only wish I knew why she killed me. You're the only person who can help me find out, and I beg you not to give up on me. I will protect you, just as I promised, if you will only allow me to do so."

Her eyes narrowed. "There's something

you're not telling me, isn't there? I summoned you, which means there must be a way for me to dismiss you. To send you back to hell, if I no longer need you."

He hadn't known it before, but something inside him knew her words to be true. He bowed low over her hand, so low he could see the floor tiles between her fingers. "Please don't send me back. I need this chance to redeem myself. To show…to show that I'm not entirely damned. That I can protect you, just like I promised to. Please, Alethia, my mistress, I beg you. I will do anything you ask."

"Stan." She tugged on her hand, trying to free it from his grasp.

He didn't dare let go. "Please," he begged.

"Stan." It sounded more urgent now, as she tugged harder. "Will you get up off the floor, please?"

Only now did he realise she wasn't trying to pull her hand free, but to pull him up.

Tears streaked her cheeks, but she was

smiling. "I'm not sure I'd ever be mean enough to want to send someone to hell, let alone you, after all you've done for me. I've known you for less than a day, and I could totally see me getting used to having you around. I think this is the first day I haven't gone completely stir-crazy, stuck in this apartment alone, since the pandemic started. Now that's all on you. In fact, if it was up to me, I'd be happy to have you stay with me for as long as you'd like. No going back to hell at all." She fixed him in her gaze, and he could feel the but hovering on the tip of her tongue. "But you need to promise me that you will protect me, and that as long as you're around, I won't be in any danger from you."

Stan's heart bloomed within his chest, almost like it was still beating, which he knew it wasn't. Alethia was the sweetest, kindest woman he'd ever met. Not to mention her beauty rivalled Carline's…

He took her in, from the graceful turn of her ankle, up her shapely leg, so clearly outlined in her tight trousers, to the swell of her hips, curving all the way up to a pair of divine breasts big enough to spill out of his hands if he were ever blessed enough to hold them. Her lips, slightly parted beneath wide, questioning eyes, as if poised to bestow a forbidden kiss…

He'd give her a thousand kisses, if she only asked for them.

And in that moment, he knew the sin that had sent him to hell. It was lust, pure and simple. He'd lusted after Carline from the moment he first saw her. Dreamed of her in his bed, or he in hers, claiming her for his own.

Alethia, twin to Carline though two centuries separated them, aroused his lust every bit as much as Carline had. More, maybe, for he'd touched Alethia, and every moment she was in his arms, the greater the temptation grew to caress her like a lover.

To steal her for his bride, as he'd hoped to steal Carline.

But he would not give in to temptation this

time, Stan told himself. He would be a paragon of virtue, instead of a lust-filled demon, and that was how he'd earn redemption. By protecting Alethia from everyone else…as well as himself.

"Stan? Answer me, please. Am I in danger with you?"

As unquenchable lust burned through his body, Stan stared up into her trusting eyes. "No," he lied.

THIRTY

"Would you like to watch some more TV?" Stan asked. He looked proud of himself for remembering the correct words, and prouder still when he picked up the remote and managed to make the screen light up.

"Actually, I'd prefer to listen to an audiobook before bed. But if you want to watch something, you go ahead. If you have any questions about what you see, write them down, and I'll try to answer them in the morning," Alethia said, pushing her notepad and a pen across the table at him.

Stan frowned. "What is an audiobook?"

"A recording of someone reading the book aloud. My mum bought me the whole series in paperback for Christmas because some of the girls where she works were raving about it, but I saw it was available in audiobook, so I bought that to listen to. When I first started listening, I was at work, and dug up something disturbing, so I haven't really gone back to it. But now I know you're the scariest thing in the cemetery, and you're here protecting me, I might be brave enough to attempt it." She glanced over at the bench, but her phone wasn't on the charger. "Damn, I must have left it in my pants pocket last night. Can you help me into the bedroom? I should be able to manage from there. Everything's only a short hop from the bed."

His eyebrows shot up. "You wish for me to carry you to bed?" That Voice again, like his thoughts were going exactly where hers were.

"If it's not too much trouble," Alethia said.

He scooped her up as if she weighed nothing. "Nothing you ask is too much trouble. I am yours to command."

For a moment, she considered commanding him to join her in bed. No more than that, though, because things had to have a sort of natural progression, not to mention consent. Not that she was going to say no if he suggested…something…

"Here?" he asked, setting her down on the end of the bed.

"Sure. Can you pass me the pants I was wearing yesterday?"

Yep, there was her phone, all right, deep inside the hip pocket of her jeans. With a dead battery. Alethia swore. No audiobook for her tonight, then.

"Can you help me put this on the charger?" She considered trying to explain, but it'd be easier to show him. "Carry me back to the kitchen for a moment."

It wasn't until her phone was back on its charger and she was sitting on the bed that she realised reading the paperback was her only option now. She reached for the brick of a book.

"I can read to you, if you wish."

If he did it in That Voice, no way was she going to turn him down. But…

"It's a fantasy romance, Stan. You might not like it," she forced herself to admit.

He drew himself up. "An adventure where people bond together to forge deep relationships through their trials, on their way to a happy ending? What sort of person does not like reading such books?"

A Regency fan of romance. Well, that was a new one. "If you're sure you don't mind…"

"I read all manner of novels to my mother when she was alive. Every week, she wanted new books from the library. She liked gothic novels the best, but she enjoyed romances, too, and she said I had the best reading voice of anyone in my family."

If he'd used That Voice, Alethia wasn't surprised. Stan's mother was a lucky woman to have her own personal audiobook narrator on command, way back when.

"All right, then." She held out *A Court of Thorns and Roses*.

Stan settled into the chair beside the bed and began to read.

THIRTY-ONE

Just as he should not have joined her on the sofa earlier that afternoon, Stan knew it was a bad idea to stretch out on the bed beside Alethia as he read aloud to her. But the chair was uncomfortable and the bed was huge…and when he asked her if he might sit closer to her…

Her eyes had lit up as she chirped, "Please do," before she plumped up the pillows for him, patting the spot where she wished him to sit.

No, Stan did not have the fortitude to deny her. Especially when the bed was wide enough to keep a proper distance between them.

Well, until she began to grow drowsy, and cuddle up to him, as she had on the couch. Even with a layer of blankets between them – blankets she lay beneath, while he'd stretched out atop them – the warmth and softness of her body against his was intoxicating, heating him from the inside out, like he'd drunk an entire barrel of good Scottish whisky.

If he'd stolen Alethia as his bride instead of Carline, and he'd spent their first day wooing her instead of resisting her, he knew their first night in bed together would not have ended with a barrier of blankets between them. No, he'd have coaxed Alethia out of her flimsy pyjamas, stroked her all over, then rid himself of his borrowed trousers before plunging deep inside her. For this woman would welcome his attentions, if the way he'd wrapped her legs around his was any indication.

Perhaps she sought such closeness because she was cold. If he could but start a fire in the grate to warm the room, then she would behave less like a wanton and more like the lady he'd promised to protect. Only there was no grate, or anywhere suitable to light a fire.

There must be some technological marvel that heated the room, if he only knew where to look, for while the weather in Western Australia was warmer than what he'd known in Scotland, the winters could still be cold. A sensible man, or at least one whose cock was not growing uncomfortably hard at the proximity of the beautiful woman wrapped around his leg, would wake her and ask.

He would then obey her instructions so that he might heat the room, while she returned to her side of the bed and he vacated the room entirely, leaving temptation behind him as she slipped back into slumber.

Whereas a demon, one of hell's wickedest denizens, would take all that she offered, and push for more. He'd seduce her, drinking her pleasure as he satisfied his own, until she had no desire to banish him from her bed, let alone send him back to hell. Instead of begging, he should have…

No. He was neither demon nor sensible man, but a lost soul who still hoped to attain heaven, where surely Carline waited for him. Which meant the pleasures of Alethia's body were not for him. All he was allowed to do was protect her, and protect her he would.

He turned toward her, instead of away, coaxing his wings into the world where they might be most useful. One slid beneath her, cupping her body and the blankets to keep all the warmth in, while the other fanned out on top of her and her coverings, enclosing Alethia like the precious pearl she was. His arms he kept ruthlessly fastened to his sides, no matter how much he wanted to reach for her.

Thank God and the devil that demons did not sleep or dream, or he would likely have surrendered to his desire in the night, and done the unthinkable. As it was, he could only lay beside her, and found that the unthinkable made for very pleasant thoughts indeed.

At least with his wings around her, no other man could get near her, he told himself.

"Mine," he growled at anyone who even thought to take her from him.

THIRTY-TWO

Alethia woke several times in the night, and each time, she found herself wrapped securely in Stan's wings, just like he'd done on the couch. At some point, she'd thrown her leg over his, as if she'd seriously intended to straddle him. She edged back onto her side of the bed, hoping he hadn't noticed.

But even with the roller shutters closed, her body clock and her smartwatch told her all too soon that it was morning, and time to get up.

"C'mon, Stan, time to let me out of my cage, so I can have a shower," she said softly, pushing at the wing that pinned her to the bed. The membrane between the bone spurs was delicate and soft to the touch, but even if she tore through it, which she didn't dare do for surely that would hurt him, the bones that gave his wings shape were too thick and too close together to allow her to break free. "You don't need to protect me from the shower. Honest. The thermostat's not set hot enough for the hot water to burn me, so the worst I can do is cut myself shaving, which I'm not going to bother doing in winter when no one will see my legs anyway."

Stan shifted irritably. "I am sure that is not a detail you should share with a man who is not your husband."

Alethia grinned. "Oh, but oversharing is my thing. Besides, you're my demon protector, so you need to know as much about me as possible, the better to protect me. I should tell you about all the parts of me I shave, when I plan to go on a date with a man who might get to see them, if he's lucky."

"There will be no such assignations while I am your protector," Stan grumbled, lifting his wing just a little. "Are you sure you wish to leave the warmth of your bed? It is cold, and I could not find the magical device you use to make a room warm in the place of a fire."

"The water in the shower will warm me up just fine. And when I get out, I can show you how to work the remote control for the air conditioning. Not that I use the heating function much in winter – it's mostly a summer thing. But if you're cold…I imagine it's much colder here than what you're used to in hell, so if you need the heater, we can turn it on."

The wings vanished, as if they'd never existed. "I am not cold."

She reached over and ran a hand down his rock hard abs. "No, you're not cold. Rather hot, actually." In all senses of the word. The sudden desire to lick all the way down every ridge of the sexy demon's tummy meant there was probably something wrong with her, Alethia decided. Then again, now she was staring at the clearly defined bulge in the front of the demon's jeans, as if he was not just reading her thoughts but sharing them.

Oh hell. Alethia swallowed as she dragged her eyes up to his face. His eyes were dark with desire. But desire for what?

"Would you like me to assist you in the bathroom?" he rumbled in That Voice.

YES. Fuck yes. She wanted him to back her up against the shower wall and…

She managed a weak smile. "I'm sure I'll be fine. My ankle hurts a bit less than yesterday, and the plastic stool's still in there, if I need to sit down."

Which she did, several minutes later when she was certain the cascade of the shower would hide any sounds she made. Sinking down on the little stool, her legs spread wide, her fingers drifted to where she ached for him, in ways no sensible woman should ache for a demon. Alethia couldn't remember being this wet for a man who hadn't even touched her, yet the moment he used That Voice…it was like her lady bits were desperately trying to dissolve her underwear to give him easier access.

She rubbed herself, imagining that it was Stan's thick fingers and not her own, as her breath grew short and the pleasure built until her orgasm came in a rush. Would it feel this good if Stan had stroked her, instead of having to do it all herself?

Alethia closed her eyes. If Stan seduced her, she was willing to bet every orgasm would be a thousand…no, a million times better, than the pathetic ones she gave herself.

If only…

THIRTY-THREE

When Monday morning dawned and Alethia's ankle still hurt too much to walk on, she called in sick to work and spent the week with Stan instead. The demon who was determined to protect her even from herself, it seemed, for no matter how dark his eyes grew, or how much his jeans bulged, he rarely touched her, except to carry her around the apartment, insisting that anything else would be unseemly or not appropriate or some other word that belonged in a Regency novel and not in the mouth of a hot, shirtless man whose voice kept her in a perpetual state of arousal.

It didn't help that he liked reading aloud to her, and would do so at the slightest excuse. And Alethia couldn't refuse. It was as if the sexiest audiobook narrator who'd ever lived had moved into her house, and she'd happily listen to him read the phone book until he was hoarse. Only she wanted to hear him read sex scenes, the really dirty kind. Actually, what she really wanted was for him to read and record them, so she could listen to them again when she was alone and...

Only she was never alone, except in the bathroom, for Stan was never out of arm's reach. Half a dozen times, she'd considered telling him to leave her alone, but it would be like kicking a puppy. A particularly creative puppy who'd tried to cook dinner in the microwave for her in a metal pot. She'd been lucky the lightning show hadn't shut off the power or set off the smoke alarm.

Well, at least she knew his cooking skills were about as bad as hers.

The more time she spent with him, the more she wanted to be with him, too. If she'd met Stan on that dating app, and he'd asked her to meet up, she wouldn't have hesitated. And the first time she'd heard his voice, she'd…well, she definitely wouldn't have run away.

She'd have wanted him to order everyone out of the restaurant, so he could bend her over the table and have his wicked way with her. Over and over and over again…

She'd settle for the kitchen table here, but Stan's attention was on the TV, while she was trying, unsuccessfully, to find any other references to Carline Bell nee Steel. Burial records, property records, passenger lists, legal proceedings, official records…she swore she had the entire State Records Office collection of documents scanned into the work database from colonisation to federation, but the only additional thing she'd managed to find was a newspaper announcement about her marriage to Sean Bell.

Which was rather odd, she had to admit. She and Sean had lived exemplary lives, if the records were to be believed – never getting into trouble with the law, or having any legal entanglements with anyone else. Even the bushfire that had claimed their home of Bell Cottage hadn't swept through until two decades after her death.

They'd never bought any more property than the original land grant they'd received surrounding Bell House and Bell Cottage, though their descendants had sold off a large chunk of the farmlands to developers over the years, the last of which was in Alethia's own lifetime, for a luxury seaside retirement village. The village was only in its final stages now, a sprawling, sand-coloured two-storey structure that mushroomed out of the bushland between Bell House and the sea, clearly visible from the western veranda of Bell House. The land had been sold on the condition that no development would exceed two storeys, so as not to disrupt the visual amenity of Bell House. The developer had evidently missed that condition in the contracts he'd signed, and he'd spent years trying to fight it, first with the local government and then with the state planning commission, to no avail. There would be no high-rise developments between Bell House and the sea.

Bell House and the surrounding lands were owned and managed by the Bell Family Trust, and administered by the same D'Angelo law firm that had set up the Trust in the 19th century. All after Carline's time, bringing Alethia back to one big, fat, dead end.

She blew out a breath. She wasn't sure which was more frustrating – her search for the woman who'd killed Stan, or his strange sense of honour that kept his pants firmly fastened.

"Is something the matter? Did you find something in your research about Carline?"

Alethia looked up to find Stan's eyes fixed on her, instead of on the paused TV screen behind him. He was watching *Grease*, one of Mum's favourites. If he liked that, maybe she should suggest *Moulin Rouge* next. Sure, she'd probably have to answer a fair few questions about it, but it'd be worth it for the moment he realised he was watching a movie about a brothel…

"What's wrong?"

She blinked. She'd better get her head out of the bordello and back into the present. But she couldn't seem to drag her gaze away from the TV screen without a twinge of envy. "You know what I miss most about being stuck in this apartment? Well, aside from sunlight, which I wouldn't be seeing much of this week even without the roller shutters, because it's raining all week, but…" Alethia coughed. Hell, her mind was wandering way too much lately. "I miss dancing. My cousins and I used to order pizza for dinner, pile into the one car, drink a six pack of beer between us on the way, and just spend the night dancing at a night club. Now, I don't even know when night clubs will be allowed to open again, or if it'll be safe to go there if they do."

"It's been a long time since I've gone dancing, too," Stan said, looking wistful.

"Then let's do it. As soon as I can find somewhere that's open, where dancing is allowed, let's go. Just you and me. Like a date," Alethia said.

"A date?" He looked confused for a moment.

Alethia took a deep breath, ready to explain.

"Oh, that's where a courting couple appear in public together, without a chaperone. For coffee or a meal or a movie, like this." Stan waved at the TV screen. "We could…"

The intercom interrupted to tell them that the grocery delivery had arrived, and Stan was soon too busy buzzing the deliveryperson up and doing his best not to threaten the man, or accuse him of anything, before helping Alethia put everything away.

By the time she was done explaining what the readymade stir-fry, pasta and curry and rice packs actually were, and that she liked these "strange foreign foods" very much, it was time for dinner, and he almost exploded when she showed him the sushi she planned to eat, and that she would not allow him to protect her from eating seaweed and raw fish. Not that the smoked salmon was truly raw, but…

When dinner was done, she was too tired to explain anything else, so she asked Stan to take her to bed and read to her. Which he was only too happy to do, so she was soon too distracted by him delivering the hero's lines in That Voice as he got more and more intimate with the heroine, that she forgot all about dancing or dates or even *Moulin Rouge*.

THIRTY-FOUR

"That'd be the pizza," Alethia called. After a week of accepting grocery deliveries, she figured Stan could manage meeting the pizza guy without scaring the shit out of him again. Though if he did run into problems, now she'd bound her ankle up in the support bandage that had arrived in the most recent grocery delivery, she could probably hobble out there in time to help. It wasn't half as nice as being carried around by her demon protector, though.

By the time she did reach the kitchen, Stan had a box in his hands and the pizza guy was gone.

"So everything went fine?" Alethia asked.

Stan stared at the box in his hands. "He wanted to thank me. Apparently, they have a competition in the pizza store for the strangest thing to happen on a delivery. The winner gets free dinner. He delivered your order tonight in the hope that he could get a second free dinner."

Alethia couldn't help but laugh. "So did he get a second free dinner?"

Stan drew himself up. "Not from me, he did not! I seized the box from him and slammed the door in his face before he could think to take it from me! This is your dinner, not his, and I told him so!"

Poor Stan. A week in the future and he still had a lot to learn. At least he hadn't scared off the pizza delivery guy.

Alethia reached for the box. "So, should we eat?"

Stan lifted the box high above his head, out of her reach. Then he wrapped his other arm around her waist. "Not until we get there." Then he whirled her around, wings flaring, and all Alethia could see for a long moment was darkness, until they popped out in the wintry night air, with Stan's wings flapping on either side of her. The road below was a long way down.

"Stan?"

The last time he'd flown with her, she'd been very drunk and in pain. She really wished he'd given her a chance to down a bottle or two of vodka before flying with him again. Worse, he was arrowing upwards, spiralling…oh shit, she was going to be sick…

…or not, as her feet touched a flat rooftop, high above the rest of the city. Alethia dropped to her knees, expecting to hit concrete, but instead she landed on…a picnic blanket? She'd recognise that tartan pattern anywhere. Her mother brought this blanket to every picnic since forever.

"Stan?" she said, more softly with a lot less panic than the first time.

He spread his arms wide, and his wings fanned out behind him, making him look huge. "You said you wanted to go on a date, with dinner and dancing. We have pizza and beer and a space big enough to dance, though I may need your help with the music, as I don't know how to make it work." He set the pizza down on the blanket, beside…

"Is that my laptop?" Right beside the portable speaker. She'd only used it in front of him once, while doing some research and there'd been a video she'd wanted to show him, in case it jogged his memory, but it hadn't.

"You should probably eat first, before the pizza gets cold."

He'd stopped calling pizza one of her strange foreign foods, but he still eyed it suspiciously as she took a slice.

Alethia smothered a smile. You could take the Regency man out of the past, but you couldn't make him eat in the present. Pity. He'd probably like pizza, if he ever actually tasted it.

"I'm not sure I should have much of the beer. I'm unsteady enough on my feet as it is. Dancing drunk will probably end with me twisting my other ankle, so I can't walk at all."

"Trust me. I won't let you fall."

Even as the logical part of her screamed that Stan was a demon, therefore this had to be a lie…she believed him.

"So how do we do this?" she asked, looking up at him.

"Well, if you will make your laptop play the right music…"

"Oh. Right." Alethia opened her laptop. "And the right music would be…?" She was pretty sure she had a playlist with the Time Warp, the Macarena, YMCA and Single Ladies on here somewhere, but she didn't think Stan would know the right moves for any of them.

Stan blushed. He actually blushed. "I…only know one dance. We learned all of them at school, because some of the students were minor gentry who might need them one day, but I only remembered the one, because it was the one that I hoped one day I'd get to dance with…the woman I'd marry."

Worried she'd have to scour the internet for Mozart or Beethoven, or worse, she raised her eyebrows. "So what's the name of this magical courting dance you dreamed of doing?" Silently, she begged whatever powers of the universe that were listening that it would be something she'd at least heard of.

"It's…scandalous. It's probably too forward of me to ask you to dance it with me, but after the films I saw on your TV, I hoped…"

"Unless it's a naked conga line with a bunch of strangers, I'm pretty sure I'll agree to it, Stan," Alethia said.

He straightened his shoulders and raised his head. Almost…defiant. Like a man a head taller than her and built like he was actually feared her reaction. "All right. I would like to dance the waltz with you."

Alethia almost laughed. Even she knew the steps for that one. "Strauss it is, then."

Stan looked confused. "Who?"

Alethia just shook her head and clicked on the first version she found. She cranked up the volume on the tiny portable speaker as high as it would go, then hit PLAY.

She clambered to her feet, trying to remember where she was supposed to put her hands. Stan didn't help — he just circled his arm around her waist and lifted her off her feet, while his other hand closed around hers. He waited a moment for the introduction to play, before he was off, whirling her around the roof without her feet ever touching it. It was almost like flying. Well, it almost was, given his wings were extended, and it was just her and him, spinning under the stars.

She laughed aloud for the sheer joy of it. They were up so high, there was nothing but stars above in the clear winter sky. And Stan's eyes, glittering in the reflected light from the city below.

"Oh, Stan, this is…this is…" Magical. Wonderful. Perfect. All superlatives that never left her lips because she was too busy wetting them, as Stan's gaze stole her attention from everything else.

She stretched up, pressing her body along his as she looped her arms around his neck. Then she pressed her lips to his.

An instant later, Stan leaned in to return her kiss and the world stood still.

The demon of her desire kissed like he meant to steal her soul through her lips, and she would surrender it willingly if he would only continue to kiss her. Just like that. Oh, yes…

An eternity passed, or perhaps it was only a moment, but she knew they'd shared a hundred kisses, and she'd trade everything she owned for a hundred more. No, for even one more, for he was the devil's own temptation, and she was falling for him so fast nothing could stop her.

The screech of a car alarm far below broke the spell. Alethia blinked her eyes open to find she'd wrapped not only her arms but her legs around Stan, so that the mighty bulge in his pants nestled in the perfect place between her thighs, and instead of holding her around the middle, his hands cupped her arse, as though with one mighty thrust, he meant to tear through his jeans and hers and impale her.

"Yes," she breathed, tightening her hold on him.

His enormous wings flapped, lifting them into the air. "I need to take you to bed," he growled, then dived.

THIRTY-FIVE

He set Alethia on her bed, prying her limbs loose from around him so that he could go back for her things. Only to realise there was someone hammering on the front door of her apartment.

A delivery of some sort, Stan assumed, as he marched to accept it. He threw open the door and found a man he'd never seen before standing there. "Well, what have you brought her?" he asked.

The man's eyes widened. "I didn't bring anything. I came to talk to Alethia. Is she home?"

"Who are you, and what business is it of yours?"

Stan wasn't sure whether he wanted to embrace the man for stopping him from ravishing Alethia, or knock him down for the interruption. Madness gripped him, and it had dug its claws into Alethia, too, for surely no sane woman would do such a thing during a waltz…

"I'm…I'm Birger. Her boyfriend. Who are you?" The man stuck his chin out aggressively. If he did not have such a weak chin, it might have been impressive.

A boy friend? Stan had never heard of such a thing. "Alethia? There is a boy here who claims to be your friend. Is it true?"

Alethia limped into the dining room. "A boy who…no, I don't have…Birger! What are you doing here? How did you get through the security gates? You shouldn't even be here! How did you get my address?"

Dread curdled in Stan's stomach, or it would have if he still had a stomach. He wasn't sure he did. "You are the one who stalks her, though you have no permission to court her? Begone, and never return. If you so much as try to speak to her again, it will be the last thing you ever do."

The boy trembled with fear, but he had courage. Stan had to give him that. "Alethia, are you all right? Did he hurt you?"

"Begone or I shall hurt you!" Stan roared.

The boy nearly tripped over his own feet, he bolted so fast down the corridor. Stan glared at him until he rounded the corner to the stairwell and vanished from sight.

Only then did he slam the door behind him and lock it.

"He will not return," Stan said with considerable satisfaction. "See? I will protect you, just like I promised." And he would not take her to bed, no matter how much he longed for her.

Alethia offered him a small smile. "Thanks, Stan." She limped back from whence she'd come.

"I will go and fetch your things from the rooftop. Then, if you wish, I will read aloud to you," Stan said. He would also take a moment to scour the surrounding streets, to make sure her stalker truly had departed.

"Sure."

But by the time he returned, her even breathing beneath the covers told him she was already asleep, with no need for his help. So he did what he did best – he sat in the chair beside her bed, and watched over her, to keep her safe. From both that boy and his own traitorous body.

It wasn't until much later that he realised that when he'd threatened the boy, he'd sounded exactly like William, when he'd warned Stan away from Carline.

But it wasn't the same, he told himself. He was protecting Alethea. Why, that boy was the reason she'd summoned Stan to be her protector in the first place.

Whereas William…

If Carline's brother had not been such an insufferable prig, Stan might have been able to court her properly. So that she might have married him, instead of some other man, and Alethia…

Alethia would not exist, because she was the granddaughter of the other man Carline had married.

And the world would be a far poorer place for it.

A future without Alethia in it…he didn't dare consider it. Wouldn't allow it to happen, because he was her protector, and he would protect her from everything and everyone who even thought to harm her.

Because she was his to protect, and no one else's.

THIRTY-SIX

On Sunday night, when she was still limping around the house, Alethia called Jeremy. She didn't want another week off sick, but there was no way she'd make it down the stairs, let alone all the way to the dig site.

"Sorry to bother you so late, but I figured you'd want an update. My ankle's still making my life hell, so…" she began.

"Good. Well, not good, but that solves a

problem for me. With the wet weather last week, everyone had time to catch up on documentation, so everyone's catalogued their finds properly before we return to site tomorrow, along with the fine weather. What I need is someone to start writing the report. And if you're stuck working from home for another week, then I choose you." He coughed. "If you need further encouragement, I can throw in a day's pay to work on your thesis, because I know you wanted to finish off your lit review. Four days of project work, and one on your thesis."

Alethia blinked. That was almost too good to refuse. "Why me?"

Jeremy made a sound in the back of his throat that sounded almost like a growl. Nothing like Stan, of course, but still… "Our Kimberley team, which were working in the Northern Territory last week, are stuck in Kununurra for two weeks, in quarantine, before they're allowed to go to site. So I had to send some of our Perth staff up to break ground on the project while we're waiting for the proper team to be released so they can take up the reins. Which means we're short staffed here, and the crew in Kununurra have their own reports to write, so you are my last, best hope. I will even hand deliver a bulk pack of toilet paper to your house, if it'll sweeten the deal."

Alethia had to laugh at that. Who'd have thought you could bribe someone with toilet paper…until there was none to be had, of course. "I'm good for toilet paper." Thanks to Mum, who'd signed up for some sort of charity delivery service for the stuff. "But if you'll let me work from home this week, that would work really well. Plus, I'm supposed to give a talk on my lit review at uni in a couple of weeks, now they've rescheduled it and confirmed a date, so a day to start preparation on that would be nice…"

"It's a deal. Talk to Justin in the office to make sure you have access to all the project files you need." He cleared his throat. "Ah, I have to go. It's feeding time, and baby bolognese is his favourite at the moment…"

Jeremy's six month old son was definitely a handful – one he'd need both hands for. "Talk to you later then, Jeremy, and good luck." She ended the call, to find Stan staring at her. "What?"

"You say some very strange things that I struggle to understand. Why must you talk about a light review, and how far must you travel in order to reach Yew Knee? There was no place of that name in the colony in my time."

"A lit review is short for literature review. It's…a report on my research from written sources. Um, so the stuff I've found out by looking at the research that's been done before we started the excavation here at the cemetery. It's definitely not a light review. It's rather deep, quite the opposite. And uni…that's short for university. I'm doing my Doctor of Philosophy on our findings from the cemetery excavation, so I'll have to write a complete research thesis in three years' time, and likely some scholarly papers in between, but it's customary to update your research colleagues on how your project is going at certain stages, and I was supposed to do my presentation in April, with everyone else, but the event got cancelled because of the pandemic, and the restrictions have only just lifted enough for it to be rescheduled now. And as I still haven't presented, I have to go up on stage and present my research, or what the client will allow from my research, to the staff and students at the university."

"You are a scholar? And you will present your findings to the important men of your university? That is truly remarkable," Stan said.

Alethia coughed out a laugh. "The important women, too. The faculty's a pretty good split between men and women now, and students…well, I think last time they checked, the women outnumbered the men, but not by many. So it's entirely possible I'll present my findings to as many men as women, or even more women than men."

Stan just shook his head. "Remarkable. I can scarcely believe…"

"That women are allowed to be educated and be responsible for educating others?" Alethia finished for him, ready to defend her choices and the centuries of feminism that separated her from him.

"No, that you are a lady scholar. I should have guessed, with your thirst for research on your laptop, as you help me find out more about Carline, that it is not just a hobby, but a vocation for a lady in your time. I mean, a wife helping her husband with his studies, I understand, but a young lady who is not yet married…I'm sure, when you do marry, your husband will not allow…"

"Shut up. Right there."

Stan's mouth gaped open in shock.

"If I marry anyone – and I may never, which is absolutely fine in this day and age – he will not allow or forbid me to do anything. This is the twenty-first century and any man who thinks women exist only to further their own ambition don't deserve any woman's attention, ever." She tapped her finger on Stan's chest. "If you want to survive in this time, you'd better remember that. Women are people, as much as any man, and we make our own choices. Any man who tries to say otherwise should be gagged by his own testicles."

She backed up, and had to hide a smile as Stan cast a worried glance at his own unharmed groin.

"When I give my presentation at the university, you're going to come with me. You're going to be a good protector who watches and listens to everything, without saying a word, unless my life is in danger. Then maybe you'll learn a bit more about the future you've arrived in, because you'll never fit in with the people today if you can't accept women as equal to men. In fact, it might be kinder to send you back to where you came from, rather than watch you struggle.

Especially as you've scared my stalker away."

"That is not what I meant, mistress. I was only a farm boy, not a scholar or a politician, with a silver tongue to smooth away the roughness of my words. I barely understood the betters of my own time, and those of yours – yourself included, obviously – confound me completely. I am not entirely stupid, or at least, I do not mean to be. Please educate me. Help me to understand. As a scholar, you are more qualified than anyone else to teach me how to behave as I must in your time. Do not send me back. I will not fail you. I promise."

Oh hell, if she met his gaze, she was going to cry. She'd almost kicked the puppy. A six foot, rock hard, muscled and winged wall of a puppy who could melt her knickers off with a single sentence spoken in That Voice, but…

"Of course I'll help you, Stan. That's what I promised. You've held up your part of the bargain, and I'd be a horrible bitch if I didn't hold up mine."

He gasped. "You cannot say that about

yourself. I mean...that is...I would never..."

"Relax, Stan. I mean, your job just got easier. My boss is letting me work from home next week, so you can protect me from right here inside this apartment, where you can hide from the sun."

"I'm not hiding."

No, he wasn't. Not really. "Which is why you'll come to my presentation at the university. At least I'll know one friendly face in the crowd."

He ducked his head. "Will they allow me to enter? I am no scholar, and my learning was limited to the village school. Surely such eminent scholars will know I do not belong among them."

Universities and schools had changed a lot in two hundred years, and she suspected she'd enjoy Stan's surprise when he found that out.

"As long as you're wearing pants, a shirt and some shoes, and keep your mouth shut, they won't suspect a thing," Alethia said. She hoped not, anyway. And if they did...she'd just tell them he was her boyfriend, and she'd brought him along for moral support because she was nervous. Because no matter how prepared she'd be, that part would definitely be true.

THIRTY-SEVEN

"And we're really looking forward to what we might find, hidden beneath the sands of East Perth Cemeteries," Alethia finished, tapping the cursor one last time to show the final slide in her presentation before she read it aloud. "Questions?"

Usually, at least one of her cousins, if not all of them, would have squeezed into the audience and stuck their hands up to ask questions she'd rehearsed beforehand. But Tacey was working, Octavia was up north at a minesite somewhere, and Callie was at a family wedding. Someone from her dad's side of the family, not the Bell side, which was why Callie was the only one of them who'd been invited.

And while Stan would be in the audience, the only sound he made was applause as he shook his head. He had no questions for her.

"Okay, I'll change that bit in the beginning to say the first known burial, because, like you said, there were undocumented burials, as well as those that were sort of documented, but not well enough to be sure where the bodies were buried." Alethia tapped at her keyboard a moment, until she was satisfied with the new slide. "Oh, and then I need to add a bit in that slide on what we hope to find, because the records aren't complete. Which sets the scene for the empty graves we found that I can't talk about because of the nondisclosure agreement with the developer…but which I will have to include in my thesis, whether the developer likes it or not."

"Are all scholarly talks so entertaining? I could listen to you lecture for hours," Stan said.

Alethia laughed. "Hell no. I mean, I started out in medicine, because that's what my family wanted me to study and I figured seeing as I'd gotten into the course, I should at least give it a try, and then I fell asleep in a lecture on cell biology. More than one, actually. It wasn't even all that boring, but the lecturer had this monotone voice that had this almost magical power to put you to sleep after listening to him for a few minutes. Unlike your voice, which I could listen to all night."

Stan preened at the compliment. "Do you wish for me to read to you again tonight?"

All night, every night. He'd finished with the fantasy romance series, and was now working his way through Mum's extensive collection of steamy paranormal and scifi romance. Once he'd stopped stumbling over the sex scenes and really gotten into the swing of things, he had become, hands down, her favourite audiobook narrator ever. She should try to record him one day…

"Yes, please, Stan," she said, slamming her laptop shut. The presentation was tomorrow and it was ready to go. She deserved a night off.

Her pyjamas were in the wash after she'd spilled coffee down the front of them. Okay, technically she'd spat coffee down the front of them when Stan, surprised by the toaster popping, had actually jumped so high off the ground he'd clunked his head on the ceiling. Watching him flap around, trying to free his horns from the light fitting had sent her into fits of laughter, and the coffee had just been a casualty, really. Much like the poor light fitting, which now had two horn-sized holes in it that she wasn't looking forward to explaining to her parents, when they got home.

Which meant she'd be wearing one of the oversized t-shirts she used as nightgowns in summer to bed. They were also easier access, when she grew too hot and bothered by Stan's reading and had to escape for a bathroom break, where she'd only have a few minutes to take care of herself before returning to bed, and Stan's watchful gaze.

For a moment, she imagined touching herself while he watched, his gaze heating to smouldering as her pleasure grew, until he offered to…

"Are you ready for me?"

He usually gave her a moment to get changed and slide under the covers before he came in to her bedroom. Some bullshit about propriety or whatever. Well, he didn't see it as bullshit – he was protecting her, or so he said. "One sec." She stripped off her clothes, dragged on a nightie, and crawled into bed. "Okay."

In he came, book clutched to his bare chest, with an eager smile on his face as if he wanted to know what happened as much as she did. He surely wasn't hanging out for the super-sexy bits, even if he did read them so well.

Stan settled in the chair today, instead of the other side of the bed, as if he'd read her thoughts and felt it best to put a safe distance between them. One thing she'd learned in this pandemic was that social distancing sucked when you wanted to be closer to someone.

He started to read, for which he always used That Voice, and Alethia closed her eyes, savouring every word.

Surprisingly early in the book, the couple's clothes started to come off, and Stan's voice lingered on words like nipple and peak and mound, savouring phrases like wet heat and tight sheath until Alethia's lady bits ached for attention. Surely Stan wouldn't notice if she just slipped a hand between her thighs and…

THIRTY-EIGHT

Every night she did this, though she tried to hide it. When the book turned steamy, she began to squirm until finally she gave in and pleasured herself. Usually, she fled to the bathroom, hiding it from him, but now he could see her hand slide down her body, between her legs.

He might not be able to ravish her completely, but he'd be damned if he'd watch and do nothing. Why, the heroes of her favourite books would never stand by and watch, when they might replace her hand with their own.

Whereas he was here in her bedchamber, as real as Alethia herself. Every bit as capable of bringing her pleasure as the imaginary men in her books. More so, for he was here.

Of course, he'd need to know what she liked first…but he was willing to find out.

THIRTY-NINE

"Do you like that?"

Alethia froze. He was staring at her now, and she didn't dare move her hand lest she draw his attention to where it was.

"Do I like what?" she asked carefully.

He waved at the pages of the open book in his lap. "All this biting and sucking and thrusting fingers into places."

Uh, yeah, or she wouldn't be inches away

from pleasuring herself to the sound of his voice.

"Does a lady's…secret place truly taste as delicious as these men say?"

Alethia couldn't stifle the snort of laughter that escaped. "Well, all the book heroes seem to think so. I wouldn't know. I've never given oral sex to a woman before. And, before you ask, no, no man has ever gone down on me, so I don't know what I taste like, either. Men taste like eggplant or zucchini when they come, and while I don't mind my vegies, I'm not really a fan of the taste during sex. Have you ever gone down on a woman? What did it taste like?"

His eyes widened. "Me? I've never done such a thing. Taken my tongue to a lady's…secret place. Yet these ladies seem to receive so much pleasure from it…"

Alethia laughed. "Well, yeah. Most guys can't make a girl come with just their dick. They need to work for it. I mean, that's the holy grail for a girl, isn't it? Getting a guy who can give good dick. Callie's convinced they're about as rare as unicorns, and she's never met one. Whereas a guy who gives good oral or is good with his hands shows he at least knows where a girl's clit is, so it's worth a shot…"

"What in heaven's name is a clit, and what is so important about it?"

Alethia closed her eyes. Any normal man, she'd be torn between kicking him out of her bedroom for sheer ignorance, or inviting him to take a look. With Stan, every bit of her body was screaming for her to invite him. Then he'd say that would be unseemly, or improper, or one of another maddening Regency words that made her want to scream.

"I think Mum might have an anatomy text book in the office I could show you," she said, flipping the quilt to one side so she could climb out of bed.

Only to find Stan kneeling on the floor beside the bed, blocking her way. He carefully placed his hand on her knee before he looked up at her with smouldering puppy dog eyes. "Would you show me? Please?" That Voice said.

A sensible girl would have swept him aside and walked past him to get that textbook.

Alethia shimmied out of her knickers and dropped them on the floor quickly, hoping he wouldn't notice how soaking wet they were. Then she slid up the bed until her back hit the headboard. "You want to see…my…" Now who was having trouble getting the words out? She'd be damned before she called any bit of her body a secret place, though.

His cheeks reddened. "I wish not only to see, but to taste. For you are sweetness itself, and I cannot imagine you being anything but delicious." He flicked his tongue out, and it looked longer than it should be. Like it belonged to a demon, a monster, instead of a man.

As if the wings and horns and claws weren't a dead giveaway.

Claws that were now resting on both her knees, pushing her legs apart oh so slowly.

His eyes begged her. Blue eyes only a shade

darker than her own. How had she not known he had blue eyes before? The eyes of a man, not a monster.

He lifted her legs over his shoulders, his eyes never once leaving hers, as he crawled onto the bed. Then he began to trace her folds with his finger. Softly, so softly it tickled, and she squirmed under his touch, wanting more that she couldn't seem to bring herself to ask for.

"Your lower lips are wet. So very wet, just like the ladies in your books. Ready to be…fucked, is that not what their lovers say?"

Slowly, Alethia nodded. If he'd only take his jeans off…

"But first, I must find this clit. A pearl, a bundle of nerves, a nub…ah, your books have so many words for this mysterious part of yours. Something to be bitten and sucked and circled…so sensitive that the merest touch…ah."

He'd found it, all right. He knew it, too, stroking her lightly at first to gauge her reaction, then harder, until she felt her back beginning to arch, pushing her hips toward him, offering more of herself. All of herself.

"This gives you pleasure," she heard him say, as her vision began to blur. She was so close.

"Yes," she panted, desperate for him to continue. To give her the release she craved. "Oh yes!"

"But all the books say I must push my fingers inside you." His finger stroked down, deep inside her, before he joined it with a second, then a third. His fingers were thicker than most men's cocks, and she liked the feel of them inside her, if only he'd stroke her clit again. Just once would be enough to…

"And I must hook them, like this?"

She wasn't sure how, but Stan had found some spot inside her that was almost as sensitive as her clit, and he knew that, too, for his eyes drank in her expression, her reaction, her every panting breath as she arched her back higher. "Please, oh, please," she begged.

"So if I stroke you in both places at once…"

His fingers worked their magic inside her, as his thumb circled her clit. Once. Twice.

Alethia screamed.

When her wavering vision returned, all she could see was Stan sucking on his claws, one at a time, with a big grin on his face. "Sweet indeed, but I suspect you will taste sweeter still when it is not my fingers making you scream, but my tongue."

He did not wait for permission, and she was too hoarse to give it, but her back had barely come to rest fully on the bed again when she arched up so that she could grab hold of his horns, and grind herself against his wicked, wicked mouth. Oh God, she wasn't sure what he was doing with his tongue, for it seemed to be everywhere all at once, even as he sucked on her clit, but she was falling fast.

For a man who didn't even know what a clit was an hour ago, he sure was the master of hers. Of her whole body at this rate, as she thrust her hips higher, locking her ankles around his neck to keep him close. Then his fangs grazed against her and she was flying, blind, wrapped in his wings with his tongue buried deep inside her, stroking places no one else had ever touched.

She whimpered as he let her down, his tongue gliding out of her in one, long lick that circled her clit one last time before abandoning her. Even after he released her legs, setting them on the mattress, she couldn't seem to bring herself to close them. She should clean up, find her knickers, put them back on…but first she wanted more.

"Please don't stop, Stan. I want more. I want all of you," she begged. When he didn't seem to understand, she reached for his pants.

His eyes widened. "No. Do not tempt me." He turned away and marched out of the room, his wings sending a cold blast of air right into her superheated core, the opposite of what she wanted.

"Stan, wait." But he did not return.

FORTY

Stan buried his face in his hands. He should not have done it. Should not have asked her. Should not have touched her. Should not have stroked her until she'd let out that first joyful scream. Should not have enjoyed it so much he'd wanted to do it all over again, before devouring her like some maddened animal until she'd screamed his name, then offered herself up for more…

His trousers were so tight with his arousal, if she'd managed to touch him through them, he was certain he'd burst. Or the trousers would, which would be just as bad, for then there'd be nothing between him and her hot, wet, tight…oh God, he wanted her so much…

He was her protector, not her ravisher.

Those little mewling noises she made when she was about to reach the peak of her pleasure…

He was her protector!

He should be saving his claws for ripping out the throats of anyone who threatened her, not raking them gently along the wet walls of her most secret place as she writhed beneath him in unabashed pleasure.

His horns were for gouging out the eyes of those who looked at her wrong, not for her to wrap her fingers around as she guided his face between her thighs, so that he might drink her sweetness from the source.

He'd even wrapped his tail around her ankles, holding her to him, so that she could not close her legs as he devoured her, taking her with his tongue as he dared not do with his cock.

He was her protector. He should not be having such thoughts about returning to her bedchamber, spreading her legs wide, and burying himself inside her so deep he would not know where he ended and she began. And then making her scream, not once, but over and over again, until she was so drunk on pleasure she could no longer move from the bed until he lifted her from it, carrying her in his arms just as he had the first week they'd met.

Stan turned on the water in the sink, setting it as cold as it would go, before freeing his cock to thrust it into the icy hell spurting from the spout.

He was her protector. He deserved this punishment, this chill, for to accept the bliss that she offered so willingly was to accept his place in hell. For if he ravished her, even if she wished it, he would no longer be her protector.

He would be just another demon, and he'd likely be sent straight back to hell, where he belonged.

"What are you doing?"

She stood in the doorway, staring at him, still wearing nothing but a short nightgown that did little to hide her bare legs, or the temptation that lay between them.

"Trying to cool my blood," he said. Though he wasn't sure if he had blood. His cock didn't ache quite as much, though. Maybe the cold water had dulled his arousal, or perhaps it had turned him numb.

"I could have taken care of you. Could still take care of you, if you wish. Women can give head, too, you know."

Stan shook his head. "And it tastes like eggplant, you said." If anything, it cooled his ardour further.

She laughed softly. "Well, one guy did. I never did it again. Maybe demons taste different. I'd be willing to try. It's only fair, after you…and I would have…but why didn't you?"

There were tears in her eyes, he saw now. He'd hurt her somehow. Perhaps not physically, but…emotionally. Maybe.

"To lie with you would be a sin. One that would damn my soul forever. I am a demon now, but as your protector, I believe I have been given a chance to do better. To change the fate of my soul. So to take what you offer without marrying you would condemn me to hell, and possibly you as well. Some protector that would make me."

Understanding dawned in her eyes. "I'm still not sure I believe in any of that, but I gather you do, and seeing as you're actually a demon, maybe I should believe in at least some of it. I still don't see how me giving you a blowjob is bad and what you did isn't, because I can tell you, there was nothing bad about any of that. If you learned all that from books, you are one hell of a scholar, and I can say that as a student myself whose mind and body you just blew. Wow, Stan. Just…wow."

"I am a terrible protector. I don't know why you don't just send me back to hell right now."

She took a step closer. "Do you want to go back?"

"No! I never want to go back. I want to redeem myself. Maybe earn a place in…the other place…where I will see Carline again."

Sadness slumped her shoulders at the mention of Carline. "I wish I'd been able to find out more about her. There's so little about the women of the early colony, and even less about her in particular. Maybe if there is an afterlife and you do see her in it, you can ask her why she did what she did. Then maybe you could have some closure. Or maybe you could offer to do to her what you just did to me, and she's sure to forgive you almost anything after that. Though…sex probably isn't a thing in heaven, so maybe not."

Stan should have been thinking of Carline. He should have been listening to what Alethea was saying, but he could not shake the image that came to mind – of her, lying on the bed before him, begging, until he gave her exactly what she wanted. What they both wanted.

But it wasn't Carline on the bed. He could not even remember her voice, or what she looked like. No, all he could see was Alethea, hear her voice. Begging him for more.

Would it be so bad to surrender to temptation, if it meant he could stay here for Alethea's lifetime? He'd never see the sun again, but he would trade that for spending every night in her bed. Every night inside her, granting her every desire.

Better than heaven, surely.

But was one short lifetime of pleasure worth spending eternity afterward in hell?

He wished he knew. If only he remembered just how bad hell was…then he would know for sure what to choose.

One thing was certain – if he had to choose between Carline and Alethia, the ghost of his past or the glorious soft sweetness beckoning him in the present, he knew exactly what he wanted.

"Would you come to bed? Just to hold me in your wings again. I'll put my knickers back on, and you can button your pants back up. So we don't…tempt…each other again."

Nothing would stop her from tempting him. One look, one touch…and he'd never forget her taste. But he could resist temptation. He'd done it before. He could do it again.

Stan nodded, and followed her to bed.

FORTY-ONE

Alethia delivered her speech perfectly, to the applause of everyone present. True to his word, Stan had not said a word to anyone since they'd arrived in the lecture theatre, but he'd surveyed the crowd, watching for any danger to her. He might not be a very good protector, particularly with all the mistakes he'd made last night, but he intended to do his best to make up for those mistakes now. Of course, watching the crowd only made him want to talk more, because what he saw…more than anything, now, he understood why he needed to protect her. Alethia was important in a way he hadn't even begun to understand while it had been just the two of them in her parents' apartment. In this crowd, it all made sense.

When the speakers trooped down from the stage to the table where tea and coffee was served, Stan made sure he reached Alethia first.

"I know you said I shouldn't say anything, but I need to tell you something. Something important."

"Is my life in danger?" she asked.

"No, but…"

She relaxed. "All right, then. What is it?"

"That was amazing. Magnificent. Did you know you managed to hold the attention of every single person in the room, from the moment you began speaking, to the very end? No one else tonight managed that. I think one man even fell asleep, but he woke up for your talk. I didn't understand it before, because I've never seen you outside the apartment, but you truly are a scholar and a teacher. Not just because of how much you love research — though I've seen your love for that, too, while you've been helping me and working on your report on the cemetery. It's the way you tell a story, almost like magic. There's something spellbinding about you when you speak. If I were your husband..."

"Stan," she warned. "If you're going to start talking shit again, you can go stand outside until it's time to leave."

If she banished him to stand outside, it would be worth it, just to tell her. "If I were your husband, I would never allow you to stop being a scholar, your whole life long, even if I had to fight every man and woman in the university to make it so. You are remarkable, and these people are lucky to be allowed to work alongside you." He bowed deeply. "I will see myself out, and I will wait for you outside all night, if that is your wish." Then he turned to go.

"Uncle Stanley?"

There was a man staring at him. A man who looked older than he was, which made no sense, for he could not possibly be this man's uncle.

The man grinned. "It is you, I'm certain of it! You're Stanley Steel, my mother's brother, my Uncle Stanley. I'm Dunstan Stone, your oldest nephew. We received your letter telling us to come to Clarence Town to meet Mr Peel, and nothing after that, but we came out here anyway, as soon as we could. That is a whole story in itself, but I won't bore you with the details. Not yet, at least, until you've told us what happened to you, and how you're here now! You must come for coffee at Anemone's place. I insist!"

"Stan?" Alethia's worried face appeared at his elbow. "Do you know this man?"

Stan looked from her to the man. What had he said his name was? Dunstan? It seemed faintly familiar, but Stan was certain he'd never seen this man before in his life. "He says he's my nephew," Stan said helplessly. It couldn't be true. Any nephews he'd had would have to be more than a century old. Long dead, just like him.

"You were asking questions about one of your ancestors," Alethia said slowly.

Dunstan seized Stan's arm. "This man, Stanley Steel. My uncle," he said proudly. "You must come to my wife's house for coffee when this is over."

A curly-haired pregnant woman appeared at his side. His wife, Stan presumed. "Dunstan, you can't just invite strangers over in the middle of the night. Maybe we should go to a café instead. Tacey's place will still be open. We could go there. She might even have some muffins left."

"You know Tacey?" Alethia asked.

The woman laughed. "Of course. My place is across the road from her café, and I live on her muffins. Even more now I'm eating for two." She patted her belly, as if she was perfectly happy to announce her condition to everyone in the room.

Stan opened his mouth to ask her how she could be so bold about something so…

Alethia jumped in: "Tacey's my cousin. If you're a friend of hers, I'm sure we'll be perfectly safe with you. Lead the way."

Stan closed his mouth and followed the woman.

FORTY-TWO

The lights were still on at the Shut Up Café, but the CLOSED sign was clearly visible on the door as they walked past on their way to Anemone's apartment. Tacey was nowhere to be seen – probably in the kitchen, doing the washing up, Alethia decided. Good thing they'd agreed to go to this woman's house…before Stan could put his foot in his mouth and say something he shouldn't.

"Stay quiet," she hissed at him as Anemone stepped inside foyer.

Someone behind her guffawed. "Why, do you think he's going to give away that he's over two hundred years old if he isn't quiet? Like Dunstan or Torstan could blend in for more than five minutes – ha! You'll fit right in, Uncle Stan."

Alethia turned, to find a whole group of people following behind them. "Who are you?" she asked, bewildered.

The man closest behind her bowed. "I am Ben Stone, the youngest brother, and I'm an artist. Most well known for my gargoyle cartoons, where a centuries old gargoyle wakes up in the present day with a wicked case of caffeine withdrawal, and takes up residence at a coffee shop. I'm on all the socials. Viral like you wouldn't believe. And when I'm not drawing, you'll find me having hot, hard, heavy monster sex with the lovely Rochelle here." He pulled a protesting girl into his arms and bent her over for a showy kiss.

"You can't tell people that," she scolded when he released her.

"Why? This is my uncle, and there's no way he can be alive without some supernatural assistance. Right, Uncle Stan?"

"Get inside before someone hears you and we get a new media circus camped on our doorstep in the morning, looking for the Moth Man again!" a new woman hissed, shoving Ben toward the door. In the light, Alethia recognised Catena.

"If they do, call me. I had the most wicked suit made, and it arrived a few days ago. I'll put it on and give your press crew quite the show." Ben wiggled on the spot in what Alethia clearly recognised as the Macarena. "Don't worry, Uncle Stan. I can teach you so you can put on a private show for your girl here, too." He winked.

"Everybody inside, please, so I can lock up!" Anemone called.

Ben and the others trooped inside.

"Up the stairs, my apartment's the one on

the right. Catena's place is the one on the left, but I've got a better coffee maker and cookies, so we're headed to mine. Oh, and watch out for the cat. Her name's Lucky and she likes to sneak out, so try and keep her inside the house, please. She's not all that into new people, so she'll probably disappear as soon as the door's closed, but just in case…" Anemone opened the door, and a black streak raced out. Right into Dunstan's arms.

He managed to keep hold of the struggling cat while everyone hurried into the house, but once the door was shut, he gave up and let the cat loose. Instead of leaving, though, she headed straight for Stan, who'd taken a seat on the couch. After a few rubs against his shin, she vaulted into his lap and settled there, purring as she kneaded his jeans.

"Ah." Anemone stared at the cat for a long moment, before sitting opposite Stan. "So, Stanley Steel, how long have you been a gargoyle?"

"A what?" Stan and Alethia asked together.

"A gargoyle. Wings, horns, claws, tail, hard-on that lasts all night, allergy to sunlight and no need to sleep, eat or drink?" Ben said.

"But…" Stan began, his eyes widening.

Ben took the seat beside Stan and draped an arm around his shoulder. "I'll handle the explanations. You girls take care of refreshments. Not because girls are better at it…except that Anemone and Rochelle would banish us from any kitchen, for good reason."

Alethia raised her hand. "I definitely belong in the banned from the kitchen club, too." She moved to take the seat on Stan's other side.

Ben was having none of it. Which made no sense, because he definitely looked like the youngest person in the room. "Nope, I need to talk to him about you, so you're going with the girls. I promise, if he tries to tell us about life in 19th century Scotland or the Swan River Colony, we can match him, tale for tale. Besides, he's probably going to need a drink by the time we're done with him, and Anemone's the best one to make it."

Anemone tucked her arm into the crook of Alethia's elbow. "He'll be fine with them, I promise. They're mostly harmless, when they're not trying to protect me from something." She grimaced.

"Wait…they're your protectors? Demon protectors?" And she was married to one? Alethia could scarcely believe what she was hearing.

Everyone burst out laughing except Alethia and Stan.

"No, gargoyle protectors. Demons don't exist!" Dunstan burst out, amid more laughter.

Ben stopped laughing. "Yeah, they do. I met one once. At an art class. He gave me his business card in case I ever needed his services. I probably still have it somewhere." He glanced up to find everyone staring at him. "What? It was a public art class. Open to anyone. It's not like they had a sign saying gargoyles and demons weren't allowed. We had a friendly chat. Just like we're going to have with Uncle Stanley here."

Alethia swallowed. This was shaping up to be a bad idea.

"Do you want to help him? Give him his life back, and his freedom?" Anemone asked.

"Is that even possible?" Alethia choked out.

Anemone nodded. "With your help, it could be. Come with me."

Alethia followed her to the kitchen.

FORTY-THREE

"God, she's hot. Have you fucked her yet?" Ben asked.

Stan stared at him in horror, while the other men berated him for his lack of manners.

"What? She is hot. I'd like to paint her. On the beach, in a swimsuit," Ben said dreamily. Then he shook himself. "But not until the weather's warmer. Family beach picnic for Christmas at Bather's Beach. You up for it?"

When he didn't get a response, he sighed in annoyance. "All right. I'll be serious. But, seriously, breaking the curse is so much easier if you're fucking her, as Tor can tell you. One night with Catena and boom! His wings fell off and he was a new man." He frowned. "Rochelle and me were at it for ages before we broke the curse, and Anemone was carrying Dunstan's baby for months before he managed to break it. Maybe it helps if you do it in your monster form. The ladies seem to like it, too, which helps."

Stan wasn't sure what to say to this boy. "Who are you?" was all that came out.

"I told you. I'm Ben Stone. Me, Dunstan and Torstan are all your nephews. You sent our Ma and Da a letter, telling us how wonderful life was at the Swan River Colony, and how we should all come and join you, and that was it, until we arrived here and no one knew who you were, or what happened to you. Then we got cursed into being gargoyles, and woke up here. We each got assigned a lady to protect, which we did, except for Dunstan who didn't use any protection, obviously, which is why Anemone's now expecting twins. With the ladies' help, we've all managed to break the curse, and then we went looking for you. And here you are!"

"But you…you're not like me. You sound like…them." He waved in the direction the women had gone.

Dunstan laughed. "You'll have to forgive Ben. He was the first of us to wake up in the present day, and he woke up in a school, where he learned about the modern world from other boys his age."

Ben gave him a dirty look. "Teenagers at an art college, thank you very much. Boys and girls, because this is the modern day, not the dark ages when you went to school. And I'm as much a man as any of you. I've been awake for twenty-one years, but if you count the years I've been asleep, I'm closer to two hundred."

"When were you born?" Stan asked.

"1834."

Stan blinked. "That's…that's the year I died."

"Except you didn't die, because you're here now. Do you remember what happened? The night you were cursed?" Dunstan leaned forward, eager to hear his answer.

Ben pointed at his brothers. "Neither of them remember the night we were cursed. I do, because I woke up when the arsehole was cutting out my heart, and killed him instead. Was it William Pearse who cursed you, too?"

"William…Pearse?" Stan shook his head. "I've never heard that name. William Steel, maybe, but I believe it was a woman who killed me. Carline Steel, the woman I wanted to marry."

"Tell us," Dunstan demanded. "Tell us everything."

So Stan did.

FORTY-FOUR

Anemone set a cup of coffee in front of Alethea. "Where'd you get him?"

Alethea considered spinning some sort of story about meeting him on a dating app, but this seemed more like a time for the truth. "East Perth Cemeteries," she said instead.

"How?"

This bit wasn't going to sound good, even to people who believed in demons and…other things. "I went on a date with this guy, who started stalking me. When I mentioned it to Callie, she said she had a spell to summon a protector for me…"

Rochelle's eyes widened. "The girls' night Tacey tried to get me to go to? But Callie doesn't believe in magic!"

"That's what I thought, too, but she said she'd been talking to some sort of…cartoonist…" Ben. She must have been talking to Ben, Alethia realised. "Anyway, she said it would be fun to try the spell, so we went down to the cemetery where we're doing an archaeological dig, but then security came, and the others ran, but I twisted my ankle, so I distracted the security guard by calling for help to let them get away. Only…Stan appeared, and took me home."

"Flew you home?" Catena asked.

How could she possibly know that? "Yes." Alethia wet her lips. "But he said he was my demon protector. That I'd summoned him to protect me."

Anemone stared dreamily into her coffee cup. "All big and muscly and naked, ready to scoop you into his arms at the perfect possible moment? Gargoyles are amazing, aren't they? Oh, and once you get them into bed…rock hard all the way down, and all night, too." She sighed, then took a sip.

"He won't…I mean, we haven't…" Alethia stammered.

"What are you waiting for? Seriously, monster sex is amazing. I mean, once you get over the size of him, and the size is definitely a plus, it's the best sex you'll ever have. Once you've tasted monster, you'll never go back," Rochelle said.

"I would if he would, but he's just…he thinks he's a demon, and that if we do it, he'll go straight back to hell, and he'll never see whatsername again," Alethia said darkly, taking a deep draught of her coffee.

"What is her name, and what is she to him?" Anemone asked.

Alethia shrugged. "Her name was Carline

Steel, before she married Sean Bell, and became Carline Bell. She died in 1887, right here in Western Australia. She's actually one of my ancestors. Stan said he was supposed to marry her, but he also said she didn't know. The first time he saw me, he mistook me for her, and asked me why I killed him, because he thinks it was her."

Anemone looked grim. "He's in love with a dead woman…and the woman who cursed and killed him? Oh, that's messed up. Someone needs to tell Dunstan. Or Ben. Between them, they'll help him get his head straightened out and banish the killer witch, or at least help him realise what she is. He'll need to, before he can break the curse. He'll need your help, too. If you're interested in helping him, of course. I mean, the sex is phenomenal, but two hundred year old men are high maintenance. They don't know their way around a coffee maker."

"Or a microwave," Alethia chimed in. "Yeah, I promised I'd help him. I thought I'd regret making a deal with a demon, but he's been wonderful. Well, except for his sex hangups, of course."

"That's because he's not a demon. He's a gargoyle. Turning to stone in sunlight is a pretty big tell," Anemone said. "He broke my bed and we had to get a new one." She looked up to find the others staring at her. "What? We forgot to close the curtains, woke up the next morning and he was stone. So heavy he broke the bed. That's all." She grinned. "So if you help him break the curse, your Stan won't break your bed. Even better, you can take him to the beach during the day, or go out to lunch together, and he'll actually eat. Seriously, if you can break the curse, he'll be almost like a normal man again, except with…certain extra abilities. Oh, and he'll get his memories back, too. Which could be very handy for an archaeologist who specialises in the time period he was actually alive."

Yes, it would. All those reasons. But also…it would fulfil her promise to him, to help him. Maybe not in the way they'd hoped, but…was it wrong to hope she could have him, and not Carline the killer witch?

"What do I have to do to break the curse?" Alethia asked eagerly.

FORTY-FIVE

"So basically, you're holding a torch for the crazy witch who cut out your heart and cursed you to a life of eternal slavery because her brother was a snobby prick?" Ben said, shaking his head. "When you could be cuddling up to the curvy Marilyn Monroe lookalike in the kitchen, or, better yet, banging her brains out until the two of you find a way to break the curse? You have issues, dude. Serious issues.

You want my advice? Go home, forget about the crazy dead fuckers in your past, who are definitely in hell where they belong, give that girl some good dick, then come back and we'll talk about curse breaking."

"But I'm not like you. I'm a demon, not a gargoyle," Stan said.

All three men – his nephews, if they were to be believed – shook their heads.

"Do you remember everything that ever happened to you?" Ben demanded.

Stan shook his head.

"It's part of the gargoyle enslavement spell. If you break the curse, you'll get all your memories back. Do you turn to stone in sunlight?"

Stan wanted to shake his head, but he'd be lying. He'd stuck his hand in the sun once, before hitting the button to close the roller shutters. It had taken almost an hour before his hand had returned to normal. "Yes."

"Gargoyle. Demons have no problem walking around in the sun and passing for normal people. Except the eyes. Their eyes can go completely black when they're angry, or thinking something really dark. Do your eyes do that?" Ben demanded.

Stan shook his head. But he'd been so sure…

"Do you bleed when your skin is cut?"

Stan shook his head. His skin didn't cut at all.

"That's because you're made of living stone. You're a gargoyle. Demons have skin not much different to a human…and they bleed black. Face it, Uncle Stan. You're not a demon. You were a man, until some crazy murderous bitch cut out your heart and turned you into a gargoyle, and now you're Marilyn's protector."

"Alethia. Her name is Alethia, not Marilyn," Stan snapped.

"But she still makes you hard in all the right places when you look at her, am I right? When you imagine what it might be like to get her naked in someplace safe, just you and her, your hardness to her softness, and boom?"

"That's not…it wouldn't be like…" Stan felt his cheeks grow hot. He couldn't possibly be blushing. He didn't have blood, for heaven's sake. Unless Ben was wrong and he was a demon…

"I've never seen a gargoyle blush before. Hey, guys, have you ever heard of a gargoyle blushing?" Ben asked.

His brothers shook their heads.

"Looks like you might have already started to resist the curse. That's good. Awesome, even. Now, take your girl home and see if you can get blood to flow into other places, where you can actually do some good." Ben gave Stan a push. "Come back once you've given Alethia a healthy helping of your cock."

Stan wasn't sure what to make of his nephew. Of any of them, but the vulgar Ben in particular.

He didn't want to believe them.

But…

Ben sure did know a lot about gargoyles and demons, and the differences between them.

He couldn't just give up on Carline like that. He'd loved her all his life.

But if Ben was right and what he remembered of that fateful night was true, Carline had not only killed him, but she'd cursed him, turning him into this creature. Then she'd gone and married someone else. She'd never cared for him. Never even known him. Yet she'd killed him without a second thought.

Alethea would never do such a thing, kind-hearted lass that she was. All Alethea wanted was to help him, even when she did not need to do any such thing. He was her sworn protector, whether he was a demon or a gargoyle or some other kind of monster entirely. His sole purpose was to protect her.

But if he was a gargoyle, like his nephews, who had not only bedded the women they protected and lived to tell the tale, but they'd managed to break free of the curse that bound them, so they were free to live their lives as they choose. To even marry, as Anemone and

Dunstan planned to, when their babies were born.

He needed to go home with Alethea. To talk all this over with her. While he decided whether to bed her, like Ben had so indelicately put it.

FORTY-SIX

The drive home was surprisingly quiet. Alethia wasn't sure what Stan's nephews had said to him, but the stories Catena, Rochelle and Anemone had told her about helping their partners break the curse and find their place in this world, when it was so different to their own time…wow. A little voice in the back of her mind whined that these woman had truly loved their partners, and that's why they'd gone to such great lengths to help them, while Alethia couldn't possibly feel that way about Stan, or she would have already broken the curse by now, just like they had.

Alethia stomped on that voice, before putting her foot on the brake to stop at the traffic lights. She did care about Stan, and she'd promised to help him. Maybe she wasn't completely head over heels in love with him, but when he kept talking about Carline, and how much his heart still belonged to her, no bloody wonder. She didn't want to get hurt, falling for a guy who didn't love her.

But Stan would be so easy to fall for. All he'd have to do was look at her with those smouldering puppy dog eyes and say something in That Voice that made her heart (and her knickers) melt, and she'd be gone. Lost.

If only…

Haha, if only he'd take a leaf out of Ben's book. Alethia could hardly believe he was from the past, when he seemed so normal. Well, not normal exactly, but like he fitted in with modern society so perfectly, no one would guess the truth. Rochelle had even shown her Ben's video channels – the man had millions of followers for his gargoyle cartoons, and he'd only been living in the present for a matter of months. But the cartoons themselves were…well, they could have taken place in her apartment, instead of the Shut Up Café, with Stan as the gargoyle and her as the barista, because Ben had gotten the dynamic exactly right. The monster from the past, fighting to find his place in a world he didn't understand, and the strange epiphanies he had about the world that were either profound or funny or a bit of both.

"Ben was quite a character, wasn't he?" Alethia ventured.

Stan grunted.

She tried again. "I'm tempted to go find his website when I get home, and binge all his cartoons. The ones Rochelle showed me were just like…"

"When we get home, I'll give you exactly one minute from the moment the door closes to undress, before I tear all your clothes off," Stan growled.

And…there went another pair of knickers, soaked through. She didn't know what to say to that. *Fuck, yes, finally,* was the first thing that came to mind, but whatever happened to DO NOT TEMPT ME? This was totally out of character for Stan, no matter how much she wanted him. So she settled for one word: "Why?"

His gaze seemed to sear her clothes off without even touching her. "Because last night I made a terrible mistake. I ignored my own desires and yours, for the faint hope of approval from a woman who killed me before she even knew me. I don't even remember what she looks like. When I think of her, all I see is you. Spread out naked on the bed before me, for me…"

Hell, her mouth was dry. Just the sound of the naked desire in his voice. She was ready to pull over onto the side of the road, drag him into the back seat of her car and…

"So you have one minute from the moment that door shuts to save your clothing from being torn apart, for before this night is through, I will be deep inside you, and nothing will stop me from taking what I want."

She swallowed, and swallowed again. She shouldn't want what he was saying. It was so wrong, and yet sounded so right…

"When we get home, we're going to have a detailed discussion about consent, buddy, because I don't think you understand how that works," she found herself saying, even as that tiny voice inside her was screaming yesyesyesyesyesFUCKyes…

He made a derisive sound deep in his throat, almost as if he could hear that voice, too. "I understand what consent is. It's you saying yes, which you did last night, and you will again, for I know you desire me as much as I desire you."

"I said yes to experimenting with oral sex, not you tearing my clothes off, and burying yourself inside me like some mindless beast." But she totally would, especially if he asked her in That Voice. Right now, in fact…

"And that is how it will start. Yes as you open yourself to me. Yes as you wrap yourself around me. Yes as you explode with the pleasure you know I can give you. Yes to doing it again until you beg for more, just like last night. And…"

The pause stretched so long, it made Alethia ache. Ache for all that he'd said he would do, as well as what would come next. "Yes?" she prompted.

He rumbled out a laugh. "Consenting already, I see. When I claim your body with my own, there will be no need for such words. Your body will know that you are mine, and your lips will scream it for all to hear."

Maybe they should stop on the side of the road. Because she was already panting for him, and if she was going to scream like he promised, it was probably better that the neighbours didn't hear. Or the whole building…

Except that they were already pulling into the parking lot, and she'd waited long enough for this. To hell with the neighbours, and whatever anyone else thought.

She floated up the stairs, barely noticing the click of the door as it closed behind him.

"One minute, Alethia, before I make you mine," Stan growled in That Voice.

A minute was far too long.

FORTY-SEVEN

Stan stalked her, following her to the bedroom as she shed her shoes, her jacket, her shirt and her stockings, before she struggled with the strange fastening of her skirt, something called a zip.

He'd already removed his shoes and shirt along the way, but he would keep the trousers for a little longer. Until she begged him to remove them, at least.

She swore as she tugged at the zip, her eyes widening as she turned around and saw how close he stood. Alethia squeaked, then forgot about the skirt and unfastened the tiny corset she called a bra, so that her breasts spilled out, begging him to touch them.

Stan didn't care how much time had passed. He would have her, now. He picked her up and tossed her onto the bed, nodding in approval as she crawled backwards until her back pressed against the pillows, just like last night.

But unlike last night, her tight skirt kept her thighs together, preventing him from taking what she wanted to offer him. With both hands, he wrenched the skirt up to her waist, where it was no longer in his way. Her knees fell open, revealing the scrap of lace between her legs that was all that now stood in his way. He slid one claw between her skin and the offending lace, rubbing his knuckle against her wet heat as she gasped at his touch. Then a second claw, as he met her questioning gaze.

"I told you I would tear them off you," he said, as he shredded the useless piece of lace with his claws, and tossed the remains on the floor.

He lifted her legs over his shoulders, just like last night, and traced her lower lips with the tip of his claw, circling that sensitive spot she called her clit until she shivered. "Do I have your consent, Alethia?"

"Fuck, yes," she gasped. "Please, Stan."

Last night, he'd taken his time, exploring every inch of her most secret places. Now, he knew exactly what to do to make her scream. Once, twice, three times…his trousers were growing so tight, if he didn't take them off soon, he'd burst the seams. God, and the taste of her…it was driving him wild.

He licked at her lazily as he tugged off his pants, bringing her closer and closer to her next orgasm as his cock sprang free.

She must have seen it, but she was no shy maiden, to be frightened by his length and girth. "Yes, please. Give me more, Stan.

Please!"

He allowed himself one last lick, savouring her taste, before pushing her hips down against the mattress, angled just right. Then he rubbed the head of his cock against her clit, now swollen from all the attention he'd lavished upon it.

"Oh yes. Yes, please!" she begged.

"I will ruin you," he warned her. As if he had not ruined her already, by the rules of the society he'd grown up with. "I will ruin you so thoroughly, you might never forgive me. But I will claim you as my own, too, so that you will never need another man in your life or in your bed."

"I need you inside me now!" Alethia complained, wiggling her hips as though she meant to drag him inside her against his will.

"First you must say the words," he said, still stroking her with the head of his cock. Oh, she was close now. So close.

"Anything. Whatever you want," she said.

"Say you're mine." In the oldest traditions

of his people, this was at the heart of marriage. Two people said the words that bound them together, before consummating their union. No banns or brothers or anything else, but two people making a promise. It might not mean anything in the laws of this time – his nephews had said as much – but it would be enough to vouchsafe the future of his soul and hers, whether he was a demon, a gargoyle, or some other monster entirely.

Alethia's eyes regarded him, dark with desire over her beautiful breasts. Breasts he could not wait to caress. "You're mine," she said, as her hand fastened around his cock, pulling him to her.

He'd never met a woman so bold. But he loved her for it, more than ever. Stan closed his eyes, then opened them again. Perhaps this was not how the traditional words went, but times had changed, and he must move with them. He freed himself from her hand, twining his tail about her wrist to keep her from grabbing him again.

"And you're mine," he said as he thrust deep inside her.

She screamed, tight walls clenching down so hard Stan could do nothing else but savour the sensation of her searing heat, claiming him just as he claimed her.

The orgasm released its grip on her body, and she released her grip on him, so that he could move within her again. One slow thrust. Another.

"Mine," he growled as he drove deep again.

"Yes. Yes, yes, yes!"

A hundred, no, a thousand times yes, as he took her, and she welcomed him, until her pleasure built to another climax and she screamed his name. At some point, her legs slipped off his shoulders, first one, then the other, and he leaned down to bestow a thousand kisses on each of her breasts, kneading them, sucking on her nipples, until she came apart beneath him again, writhing with pleasure only he could give her.

Over and over, he took her, revelling in her

ecstasy as he shared his own with her, until she collapsed atop him, utterly spent. Her head rested on her chest, her legs splayed on either side of his, as he closed his wings around his bride, his beloved, and was finally content.

The rest of the world could go to hell, for all he cared, but he would stay right here.

FORTY-EIGHT

Alethia woke aching, both inside and out. Then she shifted and realised why. She'd fallen asleep on top of Stan, her head resting on his chest, and there was no doubting what they'd done last night, or imagining it had been a dream, because his enormous dick was still buried deep inside her, at such a perfect angle that even the slightest movement sent sparks of electricity straight into her core.

Strong hands fastened around her hips, lifting her so that she sat astride him, before his wings folded around her to hold her upright when her body threatened to lie right down again, she felt so boneless. Had they really made love for hours last night, for so long that she'd actually fallen asleep with him still inside her?

"You said when you'd rested, you wanted to ride me again, as soon as you woke. You were so determined, you would not allow me to pull out, and you made me promise…" Stan gently rocked her hips, grinding her sensitive skin against him, and a moan escaped from her lips. He rocked her again, but this time he thrust up to meet her, sending even more sparks into her core.

Though she rode him, she knew that Stan was completely in control of their lovemaking, and she didn't care. After last night, no one knew her body as well as he did, and the things he could do with it…she was pretty sure she was riding a unicorn right now, one of those rare men who gave truly amazing dick.

She found herself moving with him, so perfectly attuned to his body that it came as no surprise to hear him roar her name as she screamed his. Then she lay down on his chest again, tracing the muscles. "You're mine," she said.

Stan cupped her breast in his hand. "And you're mine."

She struggled to remember what he'd said last night, before asking her to say the words. There was something... "Why is it so important to you?"

"In ancient times, right up until I was a boy, in Scotland, it was enough to say the vows and consummate the bond for a couple to be recognised as wed, by ancient custom. I know it is different now, with priests and banns and whatever modern things must be done for a couple to marry. But I have spent weeks believing I am a demon, damned to hell for eternity, and the one thing I would not do was damn you with me, no matter how much I wanted you. Last night…I began to believe that I might not be damned, that I might not be bound for hell, but I am still not certain, and I would not risk your soul on the advice of three men I barely know. So…we both said the words, and consummated our union, so under the most ancient Scottish traditions…"

Alethia burst out laughing. "Are you trying to tell me I'm your wife? That sometime last night, in the lust fuelled haze when I demanded your dick, you married me?"

"It is not legally binding, or so I believe, and even in ancient times, you would be free to divorce me, so it is not a true marriage in that sense, but…" Stan swallowed. "It is what I would have done with Carline, if I'd had the chance. I now know that would have been a mistake, but last night was no mistake. I meant to claim you, and you claimed me, and then we…" Oh, he looked so cute when he blushed.

"We had amazing sex for half the night, and again this morning. I probably should be angry with you – I mean, tricking someone into marriage during the throes of passion is probably about as underhanded as a drunken wedding in Vegas – but as you say, it's not legally binding. More like…a betrothal, or a promise. Or saying I love you."

Stan snorted. "What we did last night was much more than simply stating my feelings for you. I love you, I wish to share your bed forever, your smile lights up my world brighter than the sun…these are all things I could say over and over and while they would be true, they are not as important as declaring we share a bond, and consummating it by joining our bodies."

She had to think about that. "So…you aren't upset that I haven't said I love you?" Yet. If he truly had forgotten Carline to sort-of marry her, she was pretty sure she was in danger of falling totally head over heels in love with him. If she hadn't already, sometime during the night.

Stan shrugged. "You will say the words if

you want to, or you will not. But your eyes and your body have told me many times how much you care for me. Even now, you refuse to let me go, your tight pussy holding fast to my cock tells me how much you love me."

Fuck, he was still inside her. And she didn't want to move, because he felt so good there.

"I should take a shower," she said. So she could think. So much had happened...

"I should come with you," he said, rising with her. "If only to make sure you do not try to secretly pleasure yourself in there without me. I would definitely deserve to be divorced if my bride did not trust me enough to see to her needs."

Alethia blushed. "You knew about that?"

Stan grinned. "You made noises that sounded like you were distressed. I had no choice but to check on you, just in case. And so what if I wished it were my hands between your thighs and not your own? A man is allowed to wish, is he not?"

"I wished it was your hands, too." There.

She'd said it.

"Today, they will be." Without another word, he carried her into the shower, so their lovemaking might continue.

FORTY-NINE

When Alethia managed to pry herself away from Stan long enough to actually put some clothes on, she figured she should probably do some laundry, too. Not to mention clean bedsheets...

Once she'd set off the washing machine, she headed back to the bedroom with an armload of fresh linens to remake the stripped bed, only to hear a thumping sound against the wall.

At first, she thought it might be the washing machine, but a quick check told her it was behaving itself just fine.

She returned to the bedroom. What on earth…?

It wasn't until she heard a woman's voice screaming that she understood. Andrea the accountant next door must have company, too. Company that had stayed overnight and she was still enjoying this morning. Wait, was she shouting his name?

Alethia pressed her ear to the wall, hoping it might help her hear better, but it turned out Andrea wasn't shouting a name at all. It sounded like she was screaming, "This is the way!" Not just once, but repeatedly.

What a strange thing to say during sex.

Shaking her head, Alethea headed for the kitchen, where Stan had decided to brave the coffee machine. He still eyed the toaster with suspicion, but this week's grocery order had included almond croissants, so he'd put one of them on a plate for her, which suited her just fine.

Alethia stilled. Only one plate, and one cup of coffee. Well, he still had his horns and wings, so she shouldn't be shocked, but… "I'm sorry we didn't manage to break the curse last night, Stan. Maybe if we try again tonight…"

Stan turned and grinned at her, holding out her coffee. "Sure, if you want. But I'm not sorry. Not about last night, or about still having wings and things. I have you, and you're worth more to me than food or coffee or even sunlight. The curse binds me to you, so I'm not even sure I need to break it, if it means I must protect you. Which I would do anyway, because no one is more precious to me than you." Down went the coffee on the table, and he wrapped his arms around her.

Blue eyes stared down at her, filled with love, before his lips descended on hers and Alethia felt like it was just two of them, dancing in the stars, just like the first time they'd kissed.

It was Stan who broke the kiss, but only so that he could remind her to drink her coffee before it got cold.

After breakfast, when Alethea went to shake the croissant crumbs into the bin, she realised she'd been ignoring other chores, too. "I'll just take the rubbish downstairs. Then, if you want, I can research gargoyles and demons for you, so we can put what we learned last night into perspective."

The recycling bin was threatening to overflow, so Alethea took a bin in each hand and headed downstairs to deal with them. The big wheelie bins lined a short alley beside the car park, so she emptied each of her kitchen bins into the corresponding ones that the council trucks would pick up later in the week, then turned to head back upstairs.

Only to find Birger blocking her way. Standing in the sun, where Stan couldn't come to protect her.

Fuck.

She lifted one bin in front of her, ready to

whack him with it if necessary. "I'm warning you. If you don't get out of my way and leave me alone, Stan will hunt you down. You shouldn't be here, Birger."

"Is Stan the big guy who threatened me before?" Birger asked. "Your boyfriend?"

Alethia started to nod, then realised how that would look. "He is now, but he wasn't when I was chatting to you, or the night we met. He just kind of appeared in my life, and…" And she wanted to screw him all night, then fall asleep with him inside her, so they could do it all again in the morning. She felt her cheeks grow hot. "I'm sorry."

"No, I owe you an apology. I mistakenly thought we were soul mates, destined to be together, but I was wrong. Because of you, I found my real soul mate, and…we never could have worked. Andrea and me, we're perfect for each other. We even finish each other's sentences. I knocked on her door because I was worried about you, about your new boyfriend, because I thought he'd hurt you.

You were limping, and…"

Alethia blinked. She'd been limping? Oh, right. "I twisted my ankle. Stan came over to stay with me to help me get around while it was healing. He can be…really protective sometimes." And it was really hot, too. Him growling MINE with every thrust, until she fell apart around him.

"Well, I was worried, so I knocked on your neighbour's door, to ask if she'd noticed anything suspicious. And when Andrea answered, she was wearing the exact same t-shirt I was, only she had the matching mug! We got to talking, and then one thing led to another, and…" It was his turn to blush. "Sorry if we got a bit loud last night. We're trying for a baby, you see, because we both want one and all the natural fertility books say you need to have lots and lots of sex."

She and Stan had been too busy having lots and lots of their own sex to notice, but she was hardly going to tell Birger that. Wait… "Uh…like when she screamed, 'This is the way'?''

He went bright red. "You heard that. Sorry. We might have gotten a little carried away. We'll try to be quieter next time, I promise."

"Thanks." Alethia paused. "Was that all? Will you let me through now?"

"Yeah. I just wanted to say that I'm sorry. And that I hope you find your own soul mate. I'm sorry I wasn't yours," he said as he moved aside, so she could pass.

"Apology accepted. And you know what? Maybe I will. So you don't need to worry about me. I hope you and Andrea will be very happy together." Alethea marched back up to her apartment with her head held high. It wasn't until she'd closed the door behind her that she allowed herself to sink down with her back against it and let out the laugh that had threatened to escape all the way from the bins.

"What is it?" Stan asked. "Are you all right? You should have left the rubbish until dark, so I could go and dispose of it."

Yeah, she probably should have, but then

she wouldn't have known what her neighbour shouted during sex with Justin Bieber. What did that even mean, anyway? Maybe it was something they'd gotten from the fertility books.

When she could stop laughing long enough to catch her breath, Alethia said, "It's fine, Stan. I think you really did scare my stalker away, and he won't be bothering me again." Not if he was spending every spare minute trying to make a baby with Andrea.

"That is good news. Then perhaps I will worry less about your safety when we leave the house." Stan nodded, then turned serious. "Actually, I was thinking about last night."

Alethia grinned. "So was I. If I'd known what an amazing lover you'd be, I would have tried harder to seduce you earlier."

He blinked, as if he was surprised. "Not about the sex. About…before that. About being a gargoyle and under a curse which can be broken."

Now it was Alethia's turn to frown. "But

you said you didn't care about that. That you didn't mind that we hadn't broken the curse."

"I don't mind, but I'm not the only one who needs to know about it. You see, I'm not the only demon or gargoyle or whatever you summoned that night. My cousins…they came back, too."

More gargoyles? How had Alethia not seen them?

Wait…were gargoyles the reason for all the empty graves at the cemetery? They'd found at least a dozen of them. A dozen gargoyles, flying around the city…they'd cause chaos. If they hadn't already.

"How many?" she asked.

"There were four of us. One protector for each girl."

Each girl? Four protectors, four girls… "You mean the other girls I was with that night?"

Oh hell. This was not good. If a gargoyle had stalked Callie. Or Tacey. Or gotten anywhere near Tacey's daughter, Rory. And

Octavia…she wasn't frightening by herself, but she knew people. Scary people. People who trusted her to fix their IT problems and keep their secrets, who owed her a favour.

"What happened to them? Where are they now?" Alethia asked.

Stan looked blank. "We all flew to you to answer the summons. When I spotted you, I claimed you as mine, and told them to get their own mistress. They were still flying around, trying to decide who got who, when I flew you home. I had to remind them that you were mine several times before they finally flew off after the other girls."

"So if the girls drove home, like I told them to, your gargoyle friends probably followed them?" Alethia said slowly.

Stan nodded. "Of course. As I am your protector, they each chose a girl to protect. They would not have left them."

Three poor cursed guys from the past. Stan's cousins. Which made them family. Alethia closed her eyes. "We have to help them."

"It's kind of you to offer, but there's no need. Really. I'm sure they are adequate protectors, and nothing bad will happen to your cousins. They are just as safe as you are."

Stan didn't understand. He didn't know her family. He was a Regency man who thought women needed to be protected, instead of living a life of their own making. And the girls of Bell House were, by definition, the sort who grabbed life by the balls in every way possible, until life gave them what they wanted. Stan had no idea what his poor cousins were likely to be dealing with.

"I'm not worried about my cousins, Stan, I'm concerned about yours. Especially if they've all gone to Bell House…" Oh hell, she should have gone for a visit sooner. They were probably all garden statues outside Bell House right now. With UV lamps on at night to keep the poor blokes at bay. Because if anyone knew how to deal with supernatural creatures, it was Callie. Alethea needed to brush up on her research. Gargoyles, demons…what else? Whatever she had time for, she guessed. "As soon as it's dark, I'll take you to them. Because if your cousins followed Callie and Tacey and Octavia back to Bell House…a gargoyle curse will be the least of their problems, believe me."

Stan's eyes widened. "Are they…witches, like Carline?"

"Well, we're all descended from her, so any of us could have inherited it…but I think Callie's the only one who really qualifies. She can curse you something wicked…and she's the one who worked out how to summon you all, so if anyone's a witch, she might be." A witch who didn't believe in magic. Or good men.

"One woman is truly a danger to three grown men?" Stan didn't want to believe it.

Alethia turned grim. "Callie and her curses are a danger to all men. Especially if they piss her off. And her favourite curses? You can't break them if you're not fluent in Latin or Ancient Greek."

"Then we must rescue them before she kills them," Stan said.

"Or worse," Alethia added under her breath.

ABOUT THE AUTHOR

Demelza Carlton has always loved the ocean, but on her first snorkelling trip she found she was afraid of fish.

She has since swum with sea lions, sharks and sea cucumbers and stood on spray drenched cliffs over a seething sea as a seven-metre cyclonic swell surged in, shattering a shipwreck below.

Demelza now lives in Perth, Western Australia, the shark attack capital of the world.

The *Ocean's Gift* series was her first foray into fiction, followed by her suspense thriller *Nightmares* trilogy. She swears the *Mel Goes to Hell* series ambushed her on a crowded train and wouldn't leave her alone.

Want to know more? You can follow Demelza on Facebook, Twitter, YouTube or her website, Demelza Carlton's Place at:

www.demelzacarlton.com

Books by Demelza Carlton

Siren of Secrets series

Ocean's Secret (#1)
Ocean's Gift (#2)
Ocean's Infiltrator (#3)

Siren of War series

Ocean's Justice (#1)
Ocean's Widow (#2)
Ocean's Bride (#3)
Ocean's Rise (#4)
Ocean's War (#5)
How To Catch Crabs

Nightmares Trilogy

Nightmares of Caitlin Lockyer (#1)
Necessary Evil of Nathan Miller (#2)
Afterlife of Alana Miller (#3)

Mel Goes to Hell series

The Devil's Work (#1)
See You in Hell (#2)
Mel Goes to Hell (#3)
To Hell and Back (#4)
The Holiday From Hell (#5)
All Hell Breaks Loose (#6)
The Devil Goes to Heaven (#7)

Romance Island Resort series

Maid for the Rock Star (#1)
The Rock Star's Email Order Bride (#2)
The Rock Star's Virginity (#3)
The Rock Star and the Billionaire (#4)
The Rock Star Wants A Wife (#5)
The Rock Star's Wedding (#6)
Maid for the South Pole (#7)

Romance a Medieval Fairytale series

Enchant: Beauty and the Beast Retold
Dance: Cinderella Retold
Fly: Goose Girl Retold
Revel: Twelve Dancing Princesses Retold
Silence: Little Mermaid Retold
Awaken: Sleeping Beauty Retold
Embellish: Brave Little Tailor Retold
Appease: Princess and the Pea Retold
Blow: Three Little Pigs Retold
Return: Hansel and Gretel Retold
Wish: Aladdin Retold
Melt: Snow Queen Retold
Spin: Rumpelstiltskin Retold
Kiss: Frog Prince Retold
Reflect: Snow White Retold
Roar: Goldilocks Retold
Cobble: Elves and the Shoemaker Retold
Float: Enchanted Horse Retold
Steal: Forty Thieves Retold
Call: Pied Piper Retold

Feather: Swan Maidens Retold
Curse: Rose Red Retold
Cross: Three Billy Goats Gruff Retold
Weave: Rapunzel Retold
Claim: Puss in Boots Retold

Colony Universe

Cowboys and Aliens
Ghost
Vulcan
Cupid
Valentine
Prometheus
Halcyon
Poseidon
Apollo

Heart of Stone series

Broken Chains
Broken Bonds
Broken Dreams

Heart of Steel series

Stone Guardian
Stone Champion
Stone Sentinel
Stone Shadow